Al

THE ADVENTURES OF CAPTAIN JAC

Bad Altitude (short story)

Sapphire Eyes Are Smiling (novella)

The First Sin

The Second Sin (forthcoming)

NON-FICTION

Booking The Library: A Comprehensive Guide To Scheduling Performances And Programs For Authors, Speakers, Musicians & Entertainers

Charisma +1: A Guide to Convention Etiquette for Gamers, Geeks & the Socially Awkward

Charisma +1(2E): A Guide to Convention Etiquette for Everyone

FIND MORE AT
WWW.JESSICABRAWNER.COM

Tattoos on Dead Tree Flesh

The Library: Book 1

Jessica Brawner

To my amazing husband, Steven L. Sears who inspires and improves my writing every day. I love you. Thank you for being wonderful.

Author's Note

The following is a collection of short stories, but unlike a typical collection, it is intended to be read from beginning to end, in the order that the stories appear. Putting it together has been a delight, and I hope you enjoy every word.

"Welcome traveler! I am so glad you came to visit. It's quite the journey to get here, and I know that the outside of my home looks dilapidated, perhaps even a bit scary, and the steps are quite creaky. The paint is peeling, and the roof probably needs replacing as well. Many people aren't brave enough to enter once they see the state of things. Or maybe they think it's deserted. My library is well over two hundred years old! I try to keep the place in order, and patched up enough to protect my books, but it's always a challenge.

Myself? Oh, my age doesn't matter, although I do feel it at times. My joints are as creaky as those old steps. We've been meaning to get those fixed, the steps mind you, not my joints, but – we never can quite seem to find the funds. People don't visit my library as much as they used to. I do miss when people visited us all the time. They were always so excited, so full of life when they would first come up those stairs Young and old would flock to visit and leaf through the pages of my collection. Some would curl up in the window seat to read a romance or an adventure novel. Others would study stories of the past, tattoos of ink on paper, reading at the long wooden tables, frantically taking notes for some essay or another.

It all changed though, when the 'digital age' came about. Now they just look at cold screens with no life in them.

What they really wanted was to be allowed into the permanent collection. You have to earn your place there. But that's what they all want. Or they thought they did.

You're here, so I bet you know all about it. Of course you do!

But where are my manners, you've travelled so far to get here. Come this way and watch your step, the candlelight is dim in the hallway. Ah, here we are, my favorite reading room! Take a seat here next to the window. This old wingback chair might be threadbare, but it is one of the most comfortable in the entire house. Don't mind the scratch marks on the arms, sometimes people get quite excited while they're reading. Who knows? You may add some of your own.

Now tell me, what would you like to start off with? Where does your fancy take you? Your hopes? Your dreams? Your… fears?

I bet you'd like to start off with something light and relaxing, nothing too taxing after such a long journey; a little bit of candy if you will, to help you relax.

Yes! I think I know just the thing. It's just here on this top shelf – I can just reach it, no need to stir yourself. Don't mind the creaking, it's just the house settling, you'll get used to it.

Ah! Here it is! "Odd Goods" Just the thing to start you off. The light should be strong enough coming in from the window.

Go ahead, I'll get the fire going. I want to make sure you're comfortable. It's always bit chilly in here."

JESSICA BRAWNER

ODD GOODS

The goods are odd, but the odds are good. My mother's words as she put me on the aether liner bound for Io, Jupiter's closest moon, echoed in my mind. Apparently twenty-three is just too old to not be married and settled down. I can't believe I agreed to this — to be paraded around like a piece of meat at their annual wife meet. On the other hand, it does get me off planet, and I've always wanted to get to the moons.

The journey from Earth to Io was a month of mind numbing boredom but was drawing to a close. From the viewing deck of *The Aether Majestic* I could see the port laid out below us, the pink silicate sands glittering in the reflected light of Jupiter. I looked down at the glossy pamphlet on Io that was provided by the aether liner.

Io is a beautiful pink planet composed primarily of silicate volcanoes and underground lakes and caves.

There are volcanic eruptions visible from the main city of Aeos at least three times a day. Residents should remain within the protected environs of the city during the predicted eruption times to avoid dangerous situations. The city is protected from the harsh atmosphere of Io by the wave machine; a wondrous invention that purifies the air and removes the sand dust. The normal atmosphere on Io is breathable but many find it unpleasant. Air masks are recommended outside city limits. The primary industry on Io is the mining of Jupiter's aether, the farming of powder cane, and a silicates industry exporting the pink sands for a variety of uses. Tourist attractions include daily viewing of the eruptions, watching Jupiter set over the mountains, and hunting of the great sand crabs, one of the few forms of indigenous non-plant life on Io. One of the more colorful varieties of plant life includes the moon flowers; carnivorous plants standing ten feet tall with dazzling blue, plate-sized blooms that come out as the light of Calisto and Ganymede shine in the sky. They are quite common throughout the city. Please observe these blooms at a safe distance as they can be aggressive.

The captain's voice came over the announcement system, "Passengers please make their way to the debarkation lounge. The winches will be lowering in fifteen minutes."

My valise, along with the ridiculous dress my mother insisted on sending with me for the wife meet, would be taken to the hotel along with those of several other women here for the same event. I had chatted with many of them over the course of the voyage. For the most part, their stories were like mine, parents insisting that they must marry, or the occasional young adventure seeker, and a few orphans with no better prospects.

Vanya was the exception. She was coming to the wife meet on court order, having been convicted of behavior unbecoming a woman. Rumor had it she had been caught impersonating a man. On the voyage she refused to wear anything but trousers and men's shirts. Her one concession to femininity was a bejeweled comb in her silken black hair.

Making my way to the debarkation lounge, I found Vanya waiting for me just outside the doorway.

"Thené are you really going to go along with this wife meet? This is entirely ridiculous. I don't see why women have to get married at all if they don't want to — it's not like we have a population shortage."

"Are you really so quick to skip out on your sentence? Won't they come after you for that?" I asked.

"Okay fine, I suppose I have to at least show up." She rolled her eyes with annoyance.

I smiled; this was a conversation we had many times over the course of the voyage. "Van, come on let's at least *go* to the wife meet, it's not like we *have* to get married if we don't like any of the men. It'll be a chance for you to see me in the ridiculous dress my mother sent. That alone should be worth it. It'll be fun!"

She grumbled but joined me on the platform as we waited to descend. "Besides, how else am I going to get a chance to see man eating flowers and giant land crabs? We have to at least go down to the planet." I tapped the brochure against her forehead.

She laughed. "Fine then, just don't expect me to get into one of those outfits. I'll fend off any of the over eager miners that you can't handle."

"Deal. I am kind of curious to see what men with one blue eye and one red eye look like though. I think the effect would be a bit unsettling." I looked out the viewport, grabbing for the railing as the platform began its descent.

"It's when their eyes both go red that you have to be careful. They say it's an effect of the aether. Supposedly when a man is exposed to too much it can drive him mad." She leaned back against the window unconcerned with the shaking and vibrating of the platform.

The port was a hive of activity with giant clockwork clanks loading and unloading aether ships. Each one had a man inside to guide and control it; steam issued from vents in their backs, and the variety was astounding. Back on Earth something called electricity was starting to catch on, lighting houses and powering all sorts of things. Here on Io, the aether, so necessary for space travel, interfered with this newer technology.

A line of steam driven buggies waited for us outside the lounge. Vanya and I stepped into the next in line, its noisy puffing and clanking welcome after the strange silence of space. The passenger seats were luxurious black velvet and faced forward giving us an excellent view out the front. Our operator sat on a wooden stool bolted to the floor with a panel of pressure gages where he could easily see them, and four levers arrayed between him and the panel. As we followed the long line heading toward our hotel, he would throw the two levers directly in front of him in opposite directions any time we stopped.

The ride was slow. The caravan stopped at a scenic spots throughout the city to allow us time to see the sights, but the caravan masters did not let us descend from the carriages. Everything was shades of pink and red; the buildings, clothing, and landscape blended together until my eyes hurt to look at it. And there was sand everywhere.

Bubblegum pink mountains loomed over the city, stark against a sickly yellow sky. The mountains enclosed the city on all side but one. At 18:22 Io time, our driver stopped and pointed to a distant volcano. I felt the carriage vibrate and suddenly a giant cloud of blue steam and sand erupted. Against the nauseating yellow background it was a dramatic gash in the sky. As the ash fell, it sparkled from blue to all colors of the rainbow before settling into the shades of pink that covered everything.

The driver laughed at my wide-eyed wonder. "You missus must be here for the wife meet tomorrow. It's a handy thing for us men. It's how I met my wife some twenty years gone now. You ladies will get used to it once you've been here a while."

He started up the steam carriage again, pulling levers and turning knobs.

We arrived at our hotel and were shown to our suite of rooms by an obsequious host. As we had ridden together, Vanya and I were given the same suite. The sitting room furnishings were tastefully set in tones of beige and grey, with smaller bedrooms off to either side. *Thank the stars it's not pink.*

There was a crank operated speaking tube in one corner, and a child sized clank holding a tray of tea things and light refreshments standing in another. She was meticulously crafted of silver and brass, her tiny joints well-oiled and gleaming. The clockworks in her chest ticked softly like a heartbeat.

"Should you need anything, please let Clatter know," the bellhop gestured to the clank in the corner. "She should be able to help you with most requests."

Vanya smiled, "Thank you, I'm sure we'll be fine."

Unpacking was a matter of moments. Despite the month-long journey, I had packed light. The dress my mother sent along took up most of my luggage. I shook my head as I took it out of the trunk and hung it up. Vanya snickered.

"Oh, shut up you. It could be worse … it could be pink." I eyed the dress with repugnance. It was lime green with tiers of ruffles cut to look like leaves and a brown corset that resembled nothing so much as the bark of a tree.

The corset itself wasn't bad, but when paired with the skirt and my flyaway sable hair, I looked like someone had upended a tree and left its roots sticking out.

"Come on, let's go explore while it's still light out!" I said, hiding the offending article of clothing behind a closet door.

"Sounds like a great idea!" Vanya agreed, taking out a wide brim hat and shoving her hair up under it.

"Did you really get in trouble for impersonating a man?" I asked amused.

"Ah well, it wasn't so much that I was impersonating a man as it was which man I was impersonating." Her eyes turned steely, but then she laughed. "No matter, let's see what this pink planet has to offer."

As we headed for the lobby, we were accosted by one of the attendants. "And where do the young ladies think they're going this evening?" he said in a stern male voice.

I turned and was captured by the red and blue-eyed stare of the hotel lobby attendant. "Why, we thought to explore Aeos some before the light went." I smiled up at him.

"I'm afraid the young ladies are not allowed out of the hotel until after the wife meet tomorrow evening." He smiled down at me kindly and continued,

"For your own protection of course. Some of the men can be overly enthusiastic around the time of the wife meet."

"I see. Well perhaps you can direct us to the hotel library then. Or do you have any entertainments planned for this evening?"

"Of course. The library is right through that door, and we will have musicians performing in the hall in about three hours. Thank you for your cooperation, ladies." He tipped his hat and watched as I led the way to the library.

Vanya rolled her eyes. "You're going to let someone like him stop you from going out to see the city?"

"No of course not, but there are better ways than arguing loudly in the lobby. There must be a back door somewhere." I started examining the windows in the library. Each of them was either too small to climb through or had bars on the outside.

"Did you happen to notice if our windows had bars on them?" I asked after my inspection proved fruitless.

"No, I'm afraid I didn't. Let's see if there's a back door first though." She grinned. "I don't mind climbing out of windows, but I'd rather not if I don't have to."

The kitchen entrance was also guarded, as was the side door. Stymied, we returned to our room to discover that there were bars on our window; strange since we were three floors off the ground. Frustrated,

I sat in one of the suite's cushioned chairs as Vanya paced the room. "I don't like being trapped. There's no good reason for bars on a third-floor window. First floor, sure to keep vandals out; I could even plausibly see second floor... but third floor—they really want to keep us in," Vanya muttered.

Clatter tottered over to the sitting area and, in a stilted mechanical voice, asked, "Would you care for some tea?"

"No thank you. Clatter, is there a way out of the hotel?" I asked. The construct tipped her head to the side and looked puzzled.

"Well, perhaps they've had women try to escape before. I mean, I don't know about you, but I had to sign a contract saying I would attend the wife meet — though there was no obligation to choose a man if I didn't find one I liked." I propped my feet on grey silk the hassock.

"I still don't like it," Vanya fumed.

"Well, let's let it ride for tonight and see what happens at the wife meet. Since we have the time, I'm wondering if I can try on a pair of your trousers. I've never had the opportunity, but you always look so comfortable in them." I ran my fingers through my hair, loosening and combing out my braids.

"Oh, fine. Here let me get you a pair to try. I think I have some that should fit you, we're about the same size." Following her to her room, decorated in green and gold instead of the muted greys of the sitting room,

I stepped behind the modesty screen. I squeaked as a pair of light brown pants sailed over the screen and landed on my head. Slipping them on, I was surprised to find that they fit like a glove. Palms sweating and giggling nervously, I stepped from behind the modesty screen. "What do you think? They're not too... I mean... they're so form fitting. I probably shouldn't...."

"Yes. You should. Think of what your mother will say." Vanya laughed. "Thené, those look so much better on you than they do on me that I'm giving them to you," she smiled. "You should wear them tomorrow instead of that hideous dress."

"I don't think they'd let me in wearing pants. But I could wear them under the skirt and take the skirt off after we've been announced." I blushed at the daring idea.

Vanya laughed. "Okay, we'll do that then. Let's go down to the concert and see what the other women think of this place. Why don't you change back into your skirt for now."

I changed quickly, and we headed down to the main ballroom. The other ladies were milling about, their high-pitched, fluttery voices echoing in the cavernous space. No one seemed to feel that anything was amiss, so we sat and enjoyed the orchestral concert, commenting on the talent of the clockwork piano player and how it meshed nicely with the tones from the steam organ.

The next morning at breakfast, the hosts of the wife meet gave us our itinerary for the day. We would be touring one of the aether collection stations and returning around 16:00 to get ready for the evening's event.

The steam carriages were waiting for us outside the lobby. Vanya and I chose a different one this time, picking the last carriage in the procession. As we rolled along the pink streets of Aeos, the carriage operator prattled on about the importance of the wife meet to the residents here. Looking out at the streets it finally struck me—there were no women to be seen anywhere. *If they do the wife meet every year, then where are all the women who stay?* I pondered on that as we rolled toward the aether collection station.

It was an impressive structure, so tall that it pierced the protective wave barrier that surrounded the city. The fence surrounding the station seemed to be only knee high, but as we rolled closer, I could see it was nearly twenty feet tall with row upon row of beautiful plants in front of it. The carriage operator followed my gaze. "Those m'dears, are the moon flowers of Io. Beautiful to be sure, but mean. You stay a good distance away, and you'll be safe."

Through the fence I could see men encased in huge suits of metal, powered by pistons and steam, stomping around the outer yards of the aether station, moving crates, hauling canisters the size of the carriages, and loading them into ships bound for other places in the solar system.

Even at this distance the clangor of metal on metal was astounding, and below it all a steady thrumming sound filled the air.

Before we could reach the gates, a steam wagon raced across an intersection cutting through the line of carriages. The steam wagon turned itself sideways across the road. Men, faces covered by loose pieces of cloth, jumped out brandishing swords and cudgels and attacked the first several carriages in our line. Because of the way the road curved, I had an excellent view. The lead carriage was just beyond the intersection and had reached the row first row of flowers. I could hear panicked shrieks from the girls. Without warning the besieged carriage let out a volley of spikes in all directions. The spikes were propelled outwards, mowing down the attacking men. Several were flung back into the moon flowers by the impact.

The plants began thrashing and dipping towards the ground. One man, tried to crawl out of range and I saw a flower dip down, a long, barbed spike extending from its center. It speared the man through the back of the neck and drew him upwards into its petals. Long spine like teeth unfolded and closed on his head. His body thrashed, arms flailing, and after a moment his feet twitched once, and he was still.

Bile rose in my throat at the sight, and I looked over at Vanya. She was reaching for the comb in her hair and had a frightened, determined look on her face as she stared out at the attackers.

"Calm down young miss," the carriage operator said, as the entire line of carriages raised and pivoted in place, and then headed back the direction we had come. We were now in the lead carriage.

"What that was all about," I whispered to Vanya.

"I bet they don't tell us," she whispered back.

The carriage operator looked back at us, his eyebrow twitching. "Men fight young miss, sometimes they fight for good reason, sometimes they fight because they're wrongheaded or stupid. Either way, it's not an appropriate sight for young ladies. We take the job of protecting those that come for the wife meet seriously. A few years back we were less careful and … well, never mind."

"Ooh, tell us!" I begged, shaken, and wanting a distraction from the attack.

"Young miss, it is not a pretty story. A few years ago, before that year's wife meet, several of the girls were kidnapped by a … faction I guess you'd call it … of men who live out in the desert. We believe the girls were taken out and made into slaves in their camps, but we don't know for sure. These groups move around and hide out in the sand, and we were not able to find any of the girls. They attack almost every year, but since then, we take great care with security. At any sign of disturbance, we take you ladies back to a safe location." He smiled kindly. "We really do our best to ensure your safety and want you to be happy here."

I shuddered. "That's horrible. No one ever found the women?"

"Sadly no, but it was before I worked for the carriage company, so I don't know much more about it." He turned back to watching the road as the carriage trundled on.

We arrived back at the hotel, and the concierge herded us all inside quickly. The ladies from the carriages that had been attacked were led away in a different direction sobbing. That night, as I prepared for the wife meet, Vanya and I pondered the day's events.

"I have a bad feeling about this evening. What if those men try and attack again?" I twined my sable hair up searching for a pin to hold it.

"Here, use this." Vanya handed me a hairpin very like her own. "I agree. I've got a bad feeling about this evening. Be careful with this. There's a sleeping drug in the tip." She showed me how to twist the ruby on top and a small needle shot out the other end. "A woman should never be unarmed, particularly after what we saw today. I'll be taking my derringer as well."

I slid into the trousers and strapped my own knife into a calf sheath. It looked decidedly strange when paired with my dancing slippers. Then I turned to the hideous green skirt that Clatter held for me. "Help me get into this thing," I sighed.

Vanya laughed and lifted it over my head. "Arms up dearie, time to get trussed like a spring chicken. Just remember, you volunteered for this."

I groaned as the weight of it settled on my hips, weighing me down. The corset was easier, and Vanya was kind, lacing me not quite as tightly as custom demanded. She giggled.

"Oh, shut up," I laughed.

"Well, it's your funeral."

The other girls were all lined up waiting to enter the great hall. Vanya's slim fitting trousers and green embroidered vest attracted no few comments, but mostly they were used to her by now. As we were led onto the stage, a sea of blue and red eyed men, skin strangely pale from lack of true sunlight, were arrayed before us. They cheered, and the musicians started a lively tune. Before any of us could descend and be whirled into the dance, the walls started to shake and vibrate.

A ceiling tile crashed to the floor, then a chandelier. Shards of glass exploded in every direction. Women screamed, and men cried out as glass struck them. I threw my arm up to protect my eyes just as a giant hole opened in the outer wall and a clank crashed through it. Nearly twenty feet tall, the clank had cages that opened like clamshells instead of hands. Indiscriminately stepping on men as they tried to flee, it approached the stage; it's operator intent on the women there.

"Come ON!" Vanya shouted in my ear. I turned to flee with her and tripped over my skirt, falling heavily.

"Damn I knew that thing would be the death of you," she muttered. She took out her boot knife and started cutting the fabric away.

"Good thing I wore those pants underneath." I shuddered as the clank got closer.

"Come ON!" she shouted again. The clank had reached the women and was scooping them up into its basket hands. When it had six in each hand, it turned to leave. The remaining ladies were running in all directions now, as were the men. Vanya and I watched in horror as several men in burnooses, ends tied loosely over their faces with just their red eyes showing, entered through the hole, and started rounding up the rest of the women, dragging them out while fighting off the few men who had organized and were trying to stop them. Several bodies lay broken and bleeding on the floor, arms, legs, or torso crushed by the clank.

"We have to help those women," I whispered to Vanya.

'Yes, we do. Follow me." She skirted the edge of the chaos heading for the hole created by the clank. We dodged several of the burnoosed men, and Vanya shot one as he ran at us.

Edging past clumps of fighting men and screaming women we made it to the jagged opening. I tripped over chunks of concrete and rock as we scrambled through. My dancing slippers were not intended for this kind of activity. There was a haze of pink dust hanging in the air here, but once clear of the rubble it was easy to follow the giant machine. It towered above most of the buildings in this part of the city. "Do you know how to drive a steam carriage?" I asked, seeing the line of them before us.

She shook her head. "I'm afraid not. Never had the chance to learn."

"Well, now's as good a time as any." I sprinted for the lead carriage. *God, I love these pants.*

Vanya slammed the carriage door as I pushed the start button. "Hang on!" I cried. "I've read about how to do this, but never actually tried it."

The carriage lurched backward crashing into the one behind it. "Oops," I muttered. "Vanya, which way is the clank going?"

She stuck her head out the window. "Due north towards the desert," she yelled back. "It's moving fast."

Working the levers frantically, I got us headed in the right direction. Behind us, men in burnooses streamed out of the building, a half dozen or so carrying women slung over their shoulder, some firing back into the crowd. They did not appear to be coming our direction.

I levered the steam carriage into gear and shot off in the direction the clank was going. We were gaining on them, but the clank had a large head start. It reached the city's barrier before we did. Gritting my teeth, I drove the carriage through the shimmering wave and was surprised when I didn't feel anything as it passed over my skin. The air coming into the carriage became acrid with the smell of sulfur. Before us the pink silicate desert stretched for miles. The clank was pulling further away with each step of its massive stride.

The carriage was not built for driving in the desert. Within an hour the gears started to clog with sand and the wheels turned more slowly.

"Théne, don't you think we should turn back and get help?" Vanya asked.

"You heard the carriage operator this morning. They never found the last girls that were kidnapped. If we turn back now, we'll never know where they're being taken," I replied, rubbing grit out of my eyes.

The clank continued its ponderous walk. Either its operator hadn't noticed us following or didn't care.

As Jupiter rose on the horizon, the carriage ground to a halt, its pistons groaning as it tried to push itself forward. During the trek, Vanya had taken an inventory of the carriage. It had an emergency stash of blankets and air filters as well as a few canteens of liquid supplement and a pistol. I strapped the pistol on since Vanya still had her own.

"They can't be going too much further. The girls don't have air filters, and presumably they want them alive." I searched the carriage for other useful items. *Gods I can't believe we ran off into the desert. If we survive this* ....

The ground trembled beneath us as one of the distant volcanoes erupted, spewing blue and multicolored ash into the sky.

As the ash from the volcano started settling in our area, we slid the air filters over our faces and set off across Io's deserted landscape. The clank was still visible; it's bulk backlit by Jupiter. It seemed to have stopped when the volcano erupted.

The landscape glowed eerily in the dim light. The desert wasn't lifeless; there were a variety of shrub like plants, hard to make out in the dark of Io's night. Walking on the shifting sands was draining, but as the night progressed so did we. Jupiter was setting when Vanya called a halt.

"Thené, I think we're getting close. We need to rest for a few hours before we reach them, and I'd suggest doing it while it's still dark." She plunked down on the sand exhausted.

"I agree, and I don't know about you, but I'm a little worried about how we're going to get all those girls back to Aeos. They were all wearing ball gowns and slippers as I recall." I unrolled my blanket and made a hollow in the sand. "Sleep for a few hours then get back on our way?"

She nodded, taking a swig of her liquid supplement.

As Jupiter set and Ganymede rose, a soft clicking noise woke me from sleep. In the blue light of Ganymede, I could see that we were surrounded by sand crabs. The giant crustaceans were larger than an earth horse, their bodies armored and jointed, oblong with two antennae at one end, the other tapering down to a rounded point. They seemed more curious than aggressive, surrounding our small campsite at a respectful distance, and waving their antennae back and forth.

I shook Vanya awake whispering, "How much do you know about sand crabs?"

"Why?" She shook her head groggily.

"Open your eyes and sit up slowly," I whispered. "Don't scream."

That seemed to get her attention. She jumped to her feet, startling me, and the nearest of the creatures. It vanished in a cloud of sand.

"Shhh. I think they may be friendly," I cautioned. "Maybe they can take us to the camp."

"You're mad!" she hissed back.

I rose and approached the nearest of the sand crabs, holding my hands out in front of me, trying to mimic the motions of their antennae. It undulated backward, and I stopped, hands still out.

Remaining still, I tried not to flinch as the sand crab slithered forward, almost within arm's length. Its antennae bent and brushed my forehead. I got a feeling of questioning gentleness, and I squeaked in surprise. It dove under the sand, sending up a shower of pink silicate, and the other crabs did the same.

I turned to look at Vanya, "Did you feel that? That was unexpected. I wonder if they'll come back."

Her eyes were locked behind me. "Yes, I rather think they will."

Feeling the light touch of antennae against my back, and an unnatural calm I turned to look. The curious crab had returned. I reached out with a hand and touched the antennae in return. It undulated backwards again, but not as far, and waited. Approaching it slowly I extended my hand. It bumped one of the antennae against it, wrapping around in a surprisingly dexterous caress.

"Well, hello there. You seem friendly." I tried not to squirm as the creature's antennae stroked up and down my arm. An image of the desert and two figures trekking through it formed in my thoughts with a questioning air.

"Wait, you can communicate?"

The sand crab's antennae caressed the side of my face.

"Can you take us to the clank? I formed a picture of the giant clank in my mind.

It guided my hand over to its shell and indicated that I should climb up.

Shrugging I looked at Vanya. "It seems we've found a ride. Are you coming?"

She nodded, staring at the creatures with wide eyes as she gathered our blankets.

I turned back to the hulking creature. It waved its antennae at me encouragingly. I started climbing up the edge of its shiny, plated back, finding that the ridges made this easy. Vanya joined me on the creature's wide back. At the top there were two smaller ridges of bone, not visible from the ground. Looking for a place to hang on to, I grabbed them. The land crab took off like it was shot out of a cannon. Grabbing for Vanya as she slid down the side of the crab's shell, I let go of the ridges, and the creature slowed to an undulating amble.

"Are you ok?" I pulled Vanya back up to the top of the shell.

"Just a bit shaken. Warn me next time, will you?" she laughed nervously. "Okay, how do we steer?"

The crab's antennae twitched back at us, and I got an impression that I should not touch the ridges again. It took off at a more moderate pace toward the clank, still visible on the horizon. Behind us, the other crabs in the pod followed. Within half an hour, the kidnapper's camp came into view, the giant clank standing in the middle, its cages empty.

"Will you wait for us?" I touched the sand crab, picturing an image of girls atop the backs of each of the other land crustaceans.

It dipped its antennae in what I hoped was assent. After we slid down its shell, the creatures dove under the sand with just their antennae showing where they were.

Vanya and I crawled up a ridge of sand and peered down on the camp. The place crawled with unusual clockwork creations. Most looked cobbled together from spare parts that would fall apart if you sneezed too hard. Many of them bristled with improvised weapons. The tents surrounding the camp looked ragged and worn, and pink sand had settled on the fabric making them almost invisible. The women were nowhere in sight.

We watched until Jupiter rose in the sky again. In addition to the clanks, we counted twelve men. One stood guard outside a tent and was periodically relieved by another. I wriggled over to Vanya. "That must be where they're keeping the ladies," I whispered.

She nodded agreement.

"If we wait until Jupiter is high, then we can sneak around the back of the tent and get them out." I examined the camp further. "Lead the women over that ridge and get them on the sand crabs. I'll create a diversion on the other side of the camp to give you time."

"I'll wait for your signal. We're going to have to do this fast. How are we going to take out that clank?"

"I don't think we can. We didn't exactly bring any explosives with us." I started wriggling back down the dune. "Wait for my signal. I'll try and be obvious."

Working my way along the ridge of the sand dune, I crept to the opposite end of the camp. It wasn't a great plan. *I hope we don't all die. We're probably all going to die. I hope those clanks are as poorly put together as they look.*

On this edge of camp, I saw a bored looking sentry standing watch. He was grubby with sand, and he hadn't bathed in far too long. The gentle breeze wafted his stench in my direction, and I wrinkled my nose in distaste. Taking the hairpin Vanya had given me, I crawled slowly across the sand, thankful that it muffled sound. Providence was with me. As the sentry started to turn my direction a noise from the camp distracted him. Heart racing, I ran the last few yards and jabbed him with the hairpin.

Please work, please work, please work. He sank to the sand without a sound. I relieved him of his pistols and a staff. It was taller than I was, made from some lightweight, sturdy cane. He had been standing at the back of one of the smaller tents. Listening for a moment, I cut a small hole in the canvas and looked inside. It was empty except for an air filter, several bedrolls, and a stove. Slicing a hole big enough to step through, I entered.

The stove was already lit, making my job easier. Grabbing a shirt lying on one of the bedrolls, I wadded it up and stuck the end of it in the stove until it caught fire. As the tent filled with smoke, I set it next to the tent wall, thankful for my air mask. Within moments flames were creeping up the canvas. I picked up the shirt with a pair of tongs and exited through the slit in the back, carrying the flaming ball of cloth to the next tent. The smoke was starting to sting my eyes as I left the flaming remains of the shirt charring a hole in the edge of the second tent.

Someone raised the alarm, and clanks and men converged on the fire. *I hope that gives Vanya enough time!* Trying to keep the remaining tents between myself and the kidnappers, I made my way around the edge of the camp. While crossing an open space between two of the larger tents I heard another cry behind me. Turning to look, I saw one of the men pointing my direction. Several clanks broke away from fighting the fire and raced across the sandy open space.

I pointed the pilfered pistol at the group of oncoming clanks and fired. The unexpected recoil threw me back into the sand where I lay momentarily stunned. Using both hands, I took careful aim at the lead clank and fired. Its head exploded in a shower of springs and coils. The one next to it however seemed un-phased. I aimed at the second and pulled the trigger, the bullet passing harmlessly through its mesh casing and glancing off the one behind it. The barrel-like clank was quickly closing the gap between us, so I stood, grabbed my pole, and ran for the ridge. The clank grabbed my hair before I had gone even ten yards. I jerked out of the clank's grasp, taking its arm with me and losing a handful of hair in the process.

They really were that poorly put together!

More boldly now, I turned and swatted at it. My pole impacted with the clank's middle, sending vibrations through my hands and up my arms, and a few gears popped out the back.

I thwacked it harder and felt wood connect with metal, as I dodged the clank's other arm. A leg went flying and the thing toppled over, raising one of its arms and sending a dart flying my direction. I dodged and smashed its head with the end of my pole. More of the clanks had circled around, cutting off my escape. The fire was keeping most of the kidnappers busy, and it seemed to have spread beyond the two tents to ones further down the line. Ahead of me I could see the outline of the giant clank, motionless now without its operator.

I ran, aiming for the ladder that extended down its leg. Panting, I jumped for the lowest rung, caught the rough metal and pulled myself up. Somewhere I had lost my air filter. Gulping in the acrid air and coughing, I climbed, making for the operator's station in the clank's chest. The central operator's station was small, no more than an arm's span wide with buttons, levers, and pressure gages on every surface of the dim interior.

Well, I can't hide here forever! When in doubt, push buttons! Starting at the main console, if it could be pushed, pulled, switched, or levered I made sure to do so. The giant clank swung its arms, cages clacking together with large booming sounds, its feet started moving, walking backward. Dimly over the noise I could hear men shouting. The pressure gauges were inching from yellow to red. *Oops! Time to go!*

It was harder to climb down while the clank was moving. Each step jolted through my arms and legs, and I held on for dear life, the metal of the rungs cutting into my palms. As I neared the bottom of the ladder, there was a whooshing sound, and the clank's main body exploded outward, throwing me out into the desert sands in a hail of twisted metal.

Hitting the ground hard, I felt ribs snap as I went rolling through the fine sand. I must have blacked out for a moment or two. When I woke, the rain of metal and twisted shards had ended. Coughing the fine sand out of my lungs, I stood, nearly blacking out again from the pain as I stumbled in the direction of the rendezvous spot.

Vanya, if that wasn't enough of a signal then you weren't paying attention.

The clank had taken me further than I realized as I stumbled over the second sand dune and still saw no sign of the camp, the girls, Vanya, or the sand crabs. The pain from my broken ribs and bruised body was becoming unbearable, and I fell as I crested the ridge, rolling down the other side.

When I woke, I was surrounded by sand crabs, each with a girl on its back. *Oh, thank heavens.*

"Thené, can you stand?" I heard Vanya ask.

"Um … stand yes … walk, not very far," I whispered. I tried standing and gasped at the stabbing pain.

"You think you can ride one of these darlings if we go double and I hold on to you?" She gestured to her sand crab.

"I'll make it work. Help me up." I gritted my teeth as she boosted me onto the slick shell of the crab.

We made it back to Aeos, though I don't remember much of the trip, just the feeling of Vanya's arms holding me against the strange motion of the crab. We discovered the crabs wouldn't enter the area affected by the wave, so Vanya slid off and caught me as I came down, the girls sliding off their own crabs. The townsmen were milling around peering out into the desert and trying to organize a search party. They stared openmouthed as we stumbled into town. The elderly carriage operator was there and called for a doctor and carriages to transport us all.

They took us to a hotel — a different one without bars on the windows — and gave us rooms. I was ready to just pass out on the bed, but the doctor insisted on seeing to my ribs, and an attendant was drawing a bath. The Doctor pronounced my ribs fractured, wrapped them tightly and prescribed rest for a few days with only light activity. The other girls were being seen to, but I had sustained the worst of the injuries he assured me.

I really want a bath. I really don't want to move. The bed will get sand in it. I don't care. And I still wonder –where are all the women from past wife meets?

Sinking into the cloudlike softness of the bed I was almost asleep when I heard Vanya ask, "So, Thené, what world should we conquer next? They'll do anything to get us off planet at this point."

I smiled. "Let's discuss it in the morning."

The End

"I can tell from your smile that you enjoyed that one. I'm so pleased. It is a smile, isn't it? It was a good first choice, and you seem so much more refreshed. The color is coming back into your cheeks. That's a good sign. Now, while you were settling in, I made some tea and scones. No, no, don't get up. I'll set the tray down here, right next to you. I find this table is the perfect height for reading. It puts your tea and scones, within easy reach. We don't want the slightest distraction to disturb your adventures, do we?

And here's a footstool; your feet must be aching after all the walking. We're well off the beaten path these days, all the way out here in the woods.

No, no, don't fret about setting your cup on the wood, it's seen worse than anything you can do to it. Like everything here, it has its own stories to tell. And every little scratch and smudge is but a story of others like yourself, isn't it?

Drink your tea and let me find another story for you. Let's see…. There's one I'm thinking about, now where did I shelve it? Oh, don't mind that book over there. I was just getting down while you were reading the last story. It's one of my special books – you'll get to see it later.

Ah! Here it is. Of course, I put it back in the wrong section the last time someone read it. I am such a scatter-brained old woman. Sometimes I think the stories tell me where they want to go.

No matter, I've found it now. I think you will enjoy this one... "Ghost Writer"

GHOST WRITER

"Hey dude, I'm home!" Mandy called out as she opened the door from the garage.

"Great! I've almost got the cooler packed and ready to go. How long before you think we can get on the road?" I called back from the kitchen.

"I can be ready to go in about half an hour, I just need to throw a few things in a bag. Ed should be here tonight to take care of the furry four-legged kids," she replied, heading up the stairs.

I put the last of the breakfast tacos in the cooler and set it by the door before heading upstairs to grab my things. It would be nice to get up to the mountains for a few days without the pets. *I hope I'll have time to work on a few writing projects while we we're up there. I haven't been able to concentrate on this stuff in weeks. If I can just get one or two of them knocked out, then I'll be able to focus on my book deadline.*

"Come on dudette, let's load up and get out of here!" I yelled up the stairs.

Opening the door to the garage, a blast of cold air slapped me in the face. "Any idea what the weather's supposed to be like up in Breck?"

"Snow last I heard," she replied hauling her bag out the door and tossing it in the back of the truck, followed by her ski gear.

Pulling out of the garage the truck fishtailed on a thick patch of ice, making me cautious. The roads were going to be slick on the way up. Below the Eisenhower tunnel the snow was starting to come down lightly, just enough to wet the windshield. For a Friday going up to ski country traffic wasn't too bad. *So glad the traffic's ok. We should be there in about… two hours it looks like. Sam said last week it took him nearly eight with the crazy drivers.* The clock was reading ten past six when we pulled into the hostel parking lot.

"Let's check in and then we'll find some dinner," Mandy grabbed a couple of the bags out of the back.

"Sure, that sounds great," I grabbed my bag and followed her in. I *wonder how Mandy found this place, it's a little off the beaten track.* The door to the hostel let out into a narrow hallway with ski and snowboarding equipment hung neatly on racks along the wall.

We reserved two beds in the common room – it held eight to ten people but was less than half the price of a private room. "Hey, does anyone know where the Orion room is?" Mandy asked the room at large.

"Yeah mate, up the stairs as far as you can go, at the top of the house," a guy with dreadlocks watching the TV called back over his shoulder.

"Thanks dude," she made her way up the stairs, with me close on her heels. "I've never stayed up here before, I guess they have more than one common room."

We came to a locked door at the top of the stairs with a placard reading Orion. She slid the key in and turned, opening the door onto more stairs. These led up to an attic loft holding eight matching beds, each with a nightstand and lamp. The two beds in the middle, with towels neatly folded at the foot, held our names. Mandy N., and Jenny C.

"Well, this is different," I grinned. "It looks like something out of Snow White and the seven dwarves. Should be fun. I hope you brought earplugs."

She laughed and stashed her stuff under the bed furthest from the door. "It's a good thing you have a sense of humor. Looks like we're sharing with six guys."

We headed back downstairs and out into the cold to find dinner. The snow was falling harder, blowing sideways and muffling sound. I turned the hood up on my coat, but it didn't help much. Cold flakes found their way down the back of my neck at every opportunity. *At least it's warmer than Boulder.*

We found a funky little seafood grill a couple of blocks off Main Street, one of the few that didn't have a two-hour wait. Over Sangria and grilled trout, we celebrated being out of Boulder for the weekend.

The décor at the bar was soothing, funky and eclectic with murals painted on the walls, a traditional mirror with carved wood scrollwork behind the bar, and row upon row of expensive bottles showcased with the spotlights. The Olympic opening ceremonies were on the television, and we watched and cheered with the rest of the crowd.

We lingered over dinner then closed out our tab and slipped and slid our way back to the hostel. The snow was coming down harder now, turning into a gale and creating a curtain of white across the town.

"I'm headed to bed, I'm wiped," Mandy yawned as we made our way up the stairs to the front door and through the common room.

"Sounds good. I'm going to grab my iPad and try and get some writing done downstairs, but I expect I won't be too far behind you," I replied.

Someone was already curled up in a bunk trying to sleep so I fumbled around in the dark looking for my stuff. *Ah, there it is.*

Downstairs there was an old Victorian lounging couch off to the side of the main room. I set myself up where I could see the little TV and could hear the conversation without being intrusive. There were at least three different foreign accents. I picked out French, Australian and something else, all talking in subdued tones with an edge of worry. The Olympics were playing in the background, but no one was watching. Occasionally, the lights would flicker out then on again.

I sat, staring at my iPad, willing my fingers to type the next scene in my short story. Going back and re-reading what I had already written helped. With infinite slowness my fingers started, the words coming painfully in drips and drabs. For some reason I just couldn't get a grip on this character. Knowing how the story was supposed to go didn't seem to help; it just didn't want to come out yet.

Focusing on my work, I was startled when something large and black moved past me. I gasped and jumped, knocking my iPad over, looking wildly around. There was a large black poodle sitting, staring at me about three feet away.

"Oh, hey guy, you're a pretty puppy," I crooned, my heart pounding wildly as I offered my knuckles for him to sniff. He started growling, low in his throat, barring his teeth. I quickly withdrew my hand, but he didn't stop. The guys across the room looked up, and their mouths fell open, eyes wide with fear.

Trying to move away from the dog I pressed further back into the couch, "Hey guys, a little help over here?" I called, a chill creeping down my neck. They shook their heads, stood and ... fled? *Oh come on, the dog's not that intimidating.*

As the dog continued to growl, I scooted to the far end of the couch. His eyes did not follow me as I moved, and he ignored me when I stood up and inched along the wall. It looked for anything like he was growling at the couch itself. I glanced back and let out a small scream.

Standing directly behind the couch near where I had been, was a figure. Neither man nor woman, it was a creature, hulking, large … and insubstantial. It looked up with a startled expression and disappeared.

My eyes widened and my jaw just about hit the floor. *What on earth?* Backing up slowly I poked my head around the corner of the common room. I saw the guys peeking at me through the doorway, one of them with a ski pole in hand, his cap askew, looked like he was going to charge into the room, eyes wide and panicked. I stifled a snicker.

"*Il est parti?*" the closest one asked, his English failing him. Luckily it was French and not one of the other languages that abounded.

"*Oui, c'est parti,*" I responded. "You can come out now."

The men filed in sheepishly, looking around the corner. "What was it mate?" one of them whispered.

"Well, I didn't get a good look, but it seemed to be an apparition of some kind. It looked about as startled by me as I was by it," I replied.

"Wait, you mean this place is haunted?" the Frenchman said, sitting down at the table.

"I have no idea, why don't we ask the owners," I turned and looked at them as they came out of the private area looking groggy.

"What's all the commotion about?" the wife asked.

"We would like to know if the hostel is haunted," I replied, looking them over.

"Um," she looked at me like I was crazy. "What have you kids been smoking? I mean, I know it's legal now, but we like to keep it clean here."

"Nothing ma'am, I assure you, we all just saw what looked like a ghost," I looked to the other travelers for confirmation, and they nodded.

"Well, how peculiar," she said. "We've never been haunted before. Perhaps it was a trick of the light."

"I'm exhausted, and apparently seeing things. I think I'll head up to bed." I nodded my goodnights to the gathered assembly. Heading up to the dorm room I pondered the events. *Whatever it was, it didn't look angry, just... startled. I wonder what it was and what it wanted.*

I lay down in my bunk, thoughts swirling in my head. Popping out my iPad and opening a new document I started a journal entry.

"What an interesting evening, a ghost of all things. And a non-human one at that..." A chill crept over me, and I pulled the covers up higher under my arms as I continued to type.

"The dog growling was what initially frightened me, I don't always care for other people's pets, much like other people's children. When I saw the apparition, I was more startled than anything. I wonder if it will come back. I wonder what it was doing." I froze as my iPad started typing on its own.

"Reading your story over your shoulder… I get lonely, and the skiers are mostly boring. Writers don't stay here very often."

I squeaked and sat upright, cracking my head against the low-sloped ceiling. "Owwww," I groaned. "That's going to leave a mark," I muttered as I rubbed the top of my head. "I must have been dreaming and typing at the same time," I muttered.

I picked up my iPad from where it had fallen and stared at the screen. I saw words forming with no help from me, "I hope your head is okay, that looked painful."

"Who are you?" I typed back, "If I go to sleep, will you be here in the morning?"

The words appeared on the screen, "I'm a ghost. We can talk in the morning if that will help you believe. I didn't mean to let you see me this evening, I was just so enthralled by your story I forgot and let myself became visible."

Taking a deep breath I typed, "Okay, I'm going to go to sleep. If you're real, meet me for coffee tomorrow morning at nine a.m. at the coffee shop across the street? I'll bring my iPad."

There was a long pause, almost enough to convince me I *was* dreaming, "I have not left this place for many years, but I will try. If I do not, pardon the phrase, *appear*, it will be because I cannot. Regardless, I will not make myself visible as it seems to cause panic."

I typed back, "Very well, if you are not there by ten a.m. I will come back here, pack up and leave."

"Sleep well then, and until tomorrow."

I closed my iPad and plugged it in.. The battery was more than half drained, and if I wasn't dreaming, I wanted it at a full charge tomorrow. My stomach was knotted in fear, and I squeezed my eyes shut, pretending to sleep, afraid both that the ghost would go, and might stay.

***

Sleep wasn't in the cards for me that night. I tossed and turned, finally warming up enough to doze lightly before dawn. Waking up around seven, well before most of my dorm mates, I took a long hot shower, courtesy be dammed. Snow was flying sideways outside the window, nearly a whiteout. Mandy was up by the time I was done with my ablutions, and I joined her downstairs for a quick bite. The table was discussing last night's events.

"Dude, why didn't you wake me up!" Mandy asked as I sat down.

"Why? It was over in like two minutes," I didn't mention the conversation the creature and I may have had. *Did I dream that? If I say anything they'll think I'm crazy.*

"Still, weird. Hey, you don't mind if I still hit the slopes today do you?" she asked.

"Not at all, after last night's little adventure I have some writing to do," I rubbed my eyes tiredly.

She nodded, taking a large bite of one of the breakfast tacos.

"I'll probably spend most of the day over at the coffee shop if you need me," I gestured with my chin towards the one across the street.

Retrieving my iPad, I headed across to *Cuppa Joe*, grabbed a latte and sat down to wait. Several deep breaths later I opened my iPad. The conversation from last night was typed out in clear lines in front of me. *Oh god, it was real.*

Promptly at nine a.m. I typed, "Hello, are you here?"

I felt a chill settle over the table, like I was sitting directly under an air vent. "Y E S"

"Do you have a name?" I typed, my keyboard clattering.

"My mother called me Petri. I am … or was, what your people call a Yeti," appeared before me on the screen.

This was like having a weird instant messaging conversation.

"Can you talk out loud?" I asked out loud, forgetting myself. The few people in the coffee shop ignored me.

"I don't speak your language, though I can read it and understand," he typed.

I'm not sure why I thought it was male, just the impression I had received.

"Can you touch things in the real world? Move them around?"

"No, not physical things. I can control electrical impulses... that's how I make words appear on your screen."

"Are you a ghost?" I shivered and sipped my latte, warming my fingers on the cup.

"Yes, I suppose. A band of hunters killed me long before this town was here. Back then I was wild and angry and hadn't seen humans before. I tried to eat them, so their killing was justified. It was a kill or be killed time. I'm not sure why I'm still here though. I remember a shimmering, shining veil that wouldn't let me pass, but I never understood it. Since then, I've been stuck in this area. I eventually got bored with being angry, then I was lonely, and there was a man with lots of books. He was alone too, so I learned to read over his shoulder as he turned the pages. He would read aloud at nights, running his finger along each line. He died many years ago now and since then I've been hanging around the hostel and town getting snatches of books here and there. I've never met anyone who created the stories though! I was so excited I got distracted and became visible. Sorry if I startled you."

I could picture his head hanging in chagrin. "I… What do you want?"

"I would love to tell you my stories. I haven't had anyone I could talk to in ages. The few times people have seen me they get scared and run away. Also, I didn't know I could use these funny machines to communicate until you showed up and I tried it."

His words got me thinking. "I bet you have quite a few stories to tell… and I'm a writer… maybe I could write your stories down and then lots of people could read them."

"Would that make me a writer too?!" he typed, the words appearing almost instantly.

"I suppose it would. You would be a ghost writer," I chuckled. "Of course, I don't live here, so communication may prove difficult…" The business side of my brain kicked in, whirling out ideas too fast for me to follow on how to market these stories.

"Could… Could I come home with you?" the words appeared slowly, hesitantly on the screen.

"Is that even possible? I thought you couldn't leave this place," I typed, a puzzled look on my face.

"I am tied to my skull, I can only go a certain distance from it," he responded.

How very Dresden. My fingers hesitated over the Bluetooth keyboard, "Do you know where it is then? If I took it with me, could you come too?"

"I think so. I can lead you to where it is at any rate, and we can find out." I saw faint edges start to appear, an outline, barely there.

"You're becoming visible again," I typed quickly.

"Sorry," he vanished. "I'm just excited and I'll have to be slightly visible if you're to follow me."

"Okay, let's do this and see if it works." I wonder what Mandy will think of my bringing a skull home with me.

"I don't want to become visible with so many people around. Go to the south end of the street then turn west. You'll hit the edge of town after about a block. I'll meet you there," he typed.

The chilled feeling vanished. I packed up my iPad, finished off my latte and headed out into the near blizzard. *I can't believe I'm doing this. Maybe I've gone mad. Mother always said I had an overactive imagination maybe she was right.* I walked for about five minutes before coming to the end of the sidewalk. Hovering above the snow, barely visible in the watery light, was the figure from the night before. He was around seven feet tall, covered in coarse white hair with arms that hung nearly to his knees. He turned and headed north along a snow packed path butting up against the mountain. The walking was much more difficult here, with snow up to my knees in some places. The Yeti turned right, into an outcropping of snow and rock and vanished. *Very funny.*

Poking around the outcropping I looked for an entrance. My hands encountered an old, rusty grate. Clearing the snow, I found the roughhewn entrance to a mine shaft with the metal gate covering it. I rattled the gate, seeing if it would give way, succeeding only in dumping snow on my head. The ghost returned, still visible and reached for the lock. Despite the apparent age of the gate itself, the lock had an electronic touch pad. It clicked open at his touch, and he barred his teeth in what I suppose was a smile. I tried not to flinch at the sight.

He led the way deeper into the tunnel, until it was too dark for me to see. Running my hands along the walls for balance, I could tell that they were becoming rougher and the path more winding. Taking out my cell phone I turned on the flashlight app and held it up. *I hope the battery holds out.* As the darkness closed in, his outline became clearer. Ahead, in the wavering beam of my light I could make out a rock fall. The yeti pointed to a small opening at the top and disappeared into the rock.

Scrambling and cursing I made it to the opening. The rocks that skittered and slid under my feet threatened to bring the whole pile down. My light shone through the hole, revealing a larger room beyond. I shifted a few of the rocks, enough so that I could squeeze through the rough opening and inched through on my belly. *This is crazy. You could die here, and no one would ever find you. You better hope this whole place doesn't collapse on you.*

The ghost was waiting for me just beyond, floating silent and eerie. The room was a vast natural cavern that glittered in the faint light of my phone. After I made it to the floor of the cavern he reached out and touched my phone. The light winked out leaving me in complete and suffocating darkness.

I gasped in panic, looking about blindly, helpless without the light. Slowly my eyes adjusted and before me was a vast glittering, luminescent cave with a dark path running through it. Gazing about in wonder I followed the ghost. He led me to a niche, almost a bier, about waist high halfway down the length of the cave. In it lay a skeleton, man shaped but with the wrong proportions. The arm bones were too long, the hands were massive, and the skull was not quite human. There were arrowheads mixed amongst the bones, and one larger spearhead made from sharp glassy obsidian.

I looked over at the ghost as I reached for the large, oblong black skull with a gloved hand. He nodded as I picked it up, a hopeful look on his face. The skull was heavier than I expected, the bone thick and sturdy. *Well at least I'm not going to break it by accident. Perhaps when I get home, I can decorate it so it's not quite so macabre. I can't believe I'm doing this.*

"Well, let's go," I said, the words echoing weirdly through the cave making me shiver. I scrambled back up the rock fall, sending shards of rock scattering and clinking below me. On the other side of the hole it was pitch black. The difference was startling, and I lost my footing, sliding partway down before I caught myself. Turning on my flashlight I made my way back out of the mineshaft, closing the grate behind me.

I took my coat off and wrapped the skull in it. The bite of the wind tore into me as I hurried back to the hostel. *Mandy's never going to believe this… Aaaand maybe I shouldn't tell her.*

The ghost had disappeared when I emerged from the tunnel. Our little adventure had taken longer than I expected, and the light was starting to fade. I arrived, covered in snow and numb with cold, though it hadn't taken long to walk the short distance.

Wrapping the skull in a towel I hid it under my bed. I took out my iPad, "Are you still here? Did it work as planned?"

"It seemed to. At least, I didn't feel any negative effects," I shivered as the words appeared on my screen.

"I need to take another hot shower and hang out with Mandy when she gets back. We're leaving tomorrow morning around ten a.m. I'll take the skull with me, and hopefully you'll come along too," I wrote.

"Okay, see you tomorrow." The air suddenly warmed around me. *I am going to have to invest in warmer clothing.*

Mandy returned, little bits of snow dripping off her, cheeks ruddy from the cold. "Hey dude, lets hop in the hot tub and then grab some dinner."

"That sounds fabulous, I'm positively frozen," I rubbed my hands together trying to warm up. "Good day on the slopes?"

"The fresh powder was amazing, but with the wind it was a little hard to see," her voice muffled as she pulled her layers off. "I'm so ready for some warm."

We relaxed in the hot tub, joined by a few other folks, the warmth seeping into my bones. I hadn't realized how cold I had become walking in the cave and then the wind. After venturing out for a quick bite with Mandy I fell into bed exhausted.

I slept late the next morning, waking with just enough time to throw my stuff together, wrapping the skull securely in my towel and shoving it to the bottom of my bag. We stopped on the way out of town to grab a quick bite and lattes before making the trek home. The car, no matter how high we turned up the heat, retained a faint chill, making me smile.

"So, dude, did you get any writing done yesterday?" Mandy deftly maneuvered around a car trying to make it up to the Eisenhower tunnel.

"Some, but more importantly I came up with some new story ideas, and that's time well spent." The snow was still coming down hard and there were cars off the road on either side of us.

"Cool! Well, we should do this again soon. I had a great time skiing and it's good to get away for the weekend."

I nodded, lost in thought. Indeed, a good weekend. Time well spent. And I'd have plenty of writing ideas for the foreseeable future.

The End

"Ah, I can see that you're finally actually relaxing and settling in and getting comfortable. Did you enjoy meeting Petri and Jen? Those two are such an unlikely friendship. I have always liked their first story. They did quite well for themselves after that little adventure.

No, no, don't get up! Those old cushions have a way of making you feel at home, don't they? It's as if the chair has a personality of its own, embracing you with the promise of rest and relaxation. There's something magical about settling into such a cozy spot with a good book – it's like being transported to another world while still feeling completely at ease. Don't fight it! Let the warmth of the moment wash over you.

You are welcome to sit there for as long as you'd like and soak it all in. That's why this is my favorite reading room. Almost like it's encouraging you to stay. You feel it, don't you? Of course you do.

Anxious for another tale? Let's see… what's a good one to follow… Actually – you enjoyed the last one so much, let's try another chapter in the same book. It's an old – well-loved book after all, that's been tucked away on the bottom shelf, waiting to be discovered by yet another curious soul.

Turn to "Petri and the Spirit Walker" – here you are. It starts on this page. I'm afraid this one is darker and more graphic than the last one. A more serious tale, but you are familiar with the main characters already. I can see that won't bother you though – you were brave enough to seek me out to begin with.

Don't forget to drink your tea before it gets cold.

PETRI AND THE SPIRIT WALKER

I leaned the tablet against the narrow edge of my glass-topped desk and rubbed my eyes, hoping to dispel the fatigue and blurry vision. The oblong black skull sitting next to my computer stared at me with sightless eyes. I ran a finger over one of the prominent brow ridges. The skull was faintly warm to the touch, almost as if it were somehow alive. It wasn't, but Petri, the ghost of a yeti, was tied to it. He and I collaborated – he would tell the stories, and I would edit them and send them to my publisher.

I sighed. *Three tablets in two months, at least I got them used, ugh.* Petri's story sales provided a small, steady income, though not enough to cover that kind of extravagance. *Of course, sticking tablets all over the house is a lot cheaper than buying laptops for the same reason. I'm glad we found a text to voice app. It makes things a lot easier.*

Pulling my blanket closer around me, and turning my heating pad up a notch, I pondered. *I hope Mandy doesn't notice how much more expensive it is to heat the house these days either. No matter how warm we set the thermostat, it doesn't get above 60 degrees. Maybe it IS broken. I wonder if Petri is messing with the thermostat electronics…*

Mandy was a great live in landlord, laid back, and fun-loving. Winter was her favorite time of year, and she liked to keep the place colder than I did anyway. She may not have noticed the temperature difference. On our last trip out to Breckenridge she went skiing, and I - I had found the skull that sat on my desk and met its inhabitant. Petri had been haunting our hostel from sheer boredom and had been in the Breckenridge area for a long time. After my initial shock at seeing a ghost, and the ghost of a yeti at that, what he had to say was interesting. He convinced me to bring him back to Boulder when we left.

I stared at the curious, oblong skull sitting on my desk and sighed again. *I really should paint it or decorate it somehow so it's not so macabre. I wonder how Petri would feel about that.*

"Petri? Are you around? I asked.

The temperature in the room dropped another notch and I could see his faint, shaggy outline wavering beside the desk. Words appeared on the tablet and its mechanical voice read without inflection, "Hi Jen! What's up? Are you ready to hear another story?"

I found it interesting that Petri could read, but not speak, and we had tried several experiments to rectify the situation. The lack of inflection from the iPad voice was strange, but I got the impression Petri was eager to tell me another story.

"Yes, Petri, I'd love to." I smiled and then a fit of coughing took over. Holding down a full-time job, a part time job, and keeping up with the writing took its toll, and I had a head cold. "How did you get the name Petri? Do yetis have names like humans do?"

"Well, hmm. My mother called me 'Petri'... that's what we called the Steller Jays, but I think she called me that because I talked too much. I..." he paused. "I don't actually remember what my given name was."

I sniffled into a Kleenex and sneezed. He looked at me. "Are you okay?"

"Just a head cold," I replied, suddenly wishing for a cup of coffee, or anything hot to drink. Making a mental note to follow up on his comment later I asked, "Is your story an adventure?"

"Well, you'll have to decide. I'd like to tell you about the only time I encountered humans while I was alive. Though I should warn you, it's not a happy story." He paused, looking at me. "Do you still want to hear it?"

"Not all stories have to be happy, Petri. Life includes a variety of emotions," I replied, rubbing my hands together to warm them. "Let me grab a cup of coffee and then you can start."

His translucent, ghostly mouth opened in a toothy grin, and I could see the painting on the wall through his gaping maw. "Very well."

I stood, loathe to leave the warmth of my heating pad, and scurried downstairs. The other benefit to living with Mandy was that there was always coffee in the pot, and it was always good coffee. I poured a cup and splashed some cream and sugar in, hurrying back to my heating pad. I settled in and the tablet started talking again, while Petri hovered beside the desk.

"How do you humans start your stories? Once upon a time, a long time ago?" The voice lacked inflection, and my neck hairs rose at the eerie quality of it as Petri started his story.

"One year, in late fall, long before humans moved into the Breckenridge area, I went exploring further down the mountain than I should. Strange weather is common in the mountains when the seasons change – snowstorms blow up without warning, there's a sudden hailstorm, that sort of thing. That day, the air crackled crisp and clear, but with a hint of snow scent. Fall weather, pleasant, and still colorful but with a bite to the wind.

I had only seen fifteen summers, young for a yeti, and with as hungry as I had been, it should have been obvious; my final growth spurt was starting. My mother, Oooma, frustrated, would just throw up her paws and send me out to forage in the tundra. That year I was holding on to the season's last warm days with all my might. The cold doesn't bother me, but I enjoy the colors and smells of the other seasons much more.

Traditionally, the forest held more dangers than the alpine tundra – that's way up above the tree line in the mountains, not much grows up there. Anyway, that day the trees were eerily still. The absence of birdsong would have been deafening, but the squirrels were having a field day yelling at something. Curious, I followed the sound and came across what looked to be a group of strange, bald yeti. Humans. I know that now, but at the time they were new to me. Not a large group, perhaps five or six in all. The only fur I could see sprouted from their head. It flowed down their backs, long and dark, but didn't look like it would keep them very warm. They wore other creature's hides; deer by the smell, one or two had the fur of the black bear draped around them, and each carried a long stick, pointed at one end.

The group followed animal tracks along a path, moving quietly and quickly. I wondered where they hailed from - yeti didn't live in the surrounding mountains as far as I knew."

I interrupted him, "So, you didn't live in the forest?"

"No, we had a cave higher up in the mountains. Our cave was near the peak, up where the snow lingers year-round, and the ground never thaws. I had come down to investigate a waterway for fresh fish and late berries, even though my parents told me not to. I wanted to get the last ones before winter."

Despite the tablet's electronic voice, I swear I heard him sigh.

"I should've listened to them. I never should have gone to the lowlands." Semi-transparent in the dim light in my room, Petri's giant paws balled into fists, and his snout contorted into a grimace.

"What happened?" I asked wrapping my hands around my coffee to warm them.

"Well, curiosity got the better of me. I had never seen anything like these creatures before. Nor could I figure out why they were carrying sticks through a forest." He paused for a moment and displayed his massive paws. "I hadn't seen weapons before either. I didn't know what the sticks were. If anything threatened my father, he would fight it off with just his paws. I figured all creatures could do the same."

Petri's paws had been strong and versatile in life, twice the size of my own hands, both muscular and dexterous. Now I could see through them, and they were useful only for manipulating the energies of the world around him.

"So, I followed them," he said, picking up the story's thread. "They walked for several days, winding through the foothills and up to the higher elevations, sometimes silent, sometimes jabbering at each other in a strange language. I was careful to stay hidden, not knowing how they might react. At night they would create a camp with a fire in the middle. I had seen forest fires of course, and they were to be feared. These people had tamed it, and the glorious glow in the center fascinated me." He paused, looking to see if he had my attention.

"One night, when they lay down to sleep, I crept into the camp to see how they had trapped the fire beast. Stepping around their prone bodies, I approached. The glowing, wavering, dancing creature appeared to be devouring a pile of wood, within a ring of rocks, but the earth was bare out to the ring. The wood crackled and popped and threw off magical little sparks. Contained like this, I wondered if it was safe to touch, so I reached out and, for a moment, it flickered around my fingers harmlessly. Then my fur caught fire and I howled as it crawled up my arm and tried to eat me." He shrugged as if to say 'what, I was young, I didn't know,' before continuing with his story.

"All around me the sleepers jumped to their feet, grabbing their sticks and yelling gibberish. Frightened, I ran into the woods. The glowing creature edged up my arm further, still trying to devour my paw as I did my best to shake it off.

My chest heaved and I gasped for air, running as fast as I could. I swatted at my arm until the fire went out, but my paw throbbed and burned. Stopping, I looked around, found a small patch of snow, and thrust my burning, aching paw into it. Tears leaked from my eyes as I felt the cold relief. The little creature had eaten the fur on the back of my arm, and red angry blisters started to form from its venom.

"Well, I won't touch one of *those* again. I wonder how they had it trapped," I said aloud to the night. Sniffling I shook my head. "Perhaps it is like the prickly nettles that don't like to be touched. And I wonder what they were yelling about. Maybe I just surprised them; I did make a lot of noise. I will go apologize in the morning." I curled up behind a large boulder; my paw still packed with snow and went to sleep.

***

Examining my paw in the morning, I could see blackened patches of skin, and red, oozing blisters. It hurt. Like nothing I had felt before, but the snow seemed to be helping. Looking up toward the mountain, I could see clouds forming just beyond the peak. Raising my snout to the wind I caught that particular, damp, heavy smell that heralds a change in the weather. It would snow in the late afternoon unless the wind shifted. Making my way back down the mountain, I snagged a few pinecones, and found some soft apples overlooked by the bears, for breakfast.

When I reached the campsite, the group looked like a herd of deer about to flee. They jumped at every sound, and their eyes widened with fear as they talked. I had trouble puzzling out what they were agitated about, but when they started walking, they followed my flight from the night before.

Nursing my wounded paw, I trailed after them at a distance, cautious and hidden, still curious, but not yet willing to approach. Truth be told, my actions of the night before embarrassed me.

After watching them backtrack my flight for a few hours, I grew bored. The trees were thin here and no underbrush hindered my movements. It was much harder to stay hidden and out of sight. I did smell the brown bear's sharp tang not far away, though he seemed concerned only with filling his belly before winter. Despite the lack of threat, the hunters twitched nervously every time a ground squirrel ran across their path.

When the sun paused in its daily trek, high overhead, I gathered my courage and decided to see if they could answer some questions.

I outdistanced them, circled around, and picked a spot along my trail to wait.

**

The leader appeared around a curve in the path in front of my hiding spot. I stepped out from behind a tree and said, "Welcome!" in the yeti tongue, raising my arms high and splaying my fingers to the heavens, but keeping my eyes locked on the group.

He shrieked, startled, and threw his stick at me. It wobbled mid-air. It hadn't been thrown very hard, so I caught it with my good paw. I threw the stick back to him, thinking perhaps they greeted people that way. The stick landed point down with a thud at his feet, swaying back and forth in the earth. It must have been the wrong thing to do. The group scattered in all directions, leaving me scratching my head in puzzlement.

They can't possibly be afraid of me. I wouldn't hurt a fly.

As I pondered, I felt a burning sensation along the back of my calf and reached down to swat at it, expecting to encounter a biting fly. They plagued this area in summer but were usually gone by late fall. My paw came away bloody. A sliver of wood with a sharp point on it lay on the ground near my heel. Something else hissed near my head, and another arrow flew overhead. A searing pain blossomed in my shoulder. Letting out a yell I ran. They were throwing things at me! And it *hurt*! I decided I wasn't *that* curious about them. Besides, it had been close to a week, my mother would be anxious. Running through the forest, dodging low-hanging branches and brambles I headed for home.

The excruciating pain in my shoulder slowed me down. Stopping to rest for a moment I reached around and discovered one of the small shafts of wood stuck out from my shoulder. I groaned and closed my eyes, steeling myself to pull it free.

It's no worse than a cougar claw, just one yank and its out, deep breaths, you can do this. Shuddering I remembered when Oooma had removed the cougar claw last year. *You're nearly an adult; you can do this.* Squinting my eyes shut and screwing my face up in a grimace, I yanked. The sliver of wood came free, and a small spurt of blood trickled out, flowing down my shoulder in a slow, steady stream, matting in my fur. *Oooma will not be pleased about this.*

After resting for a few moments, I started back toward our cave. I had at least two peaks to cross to get home. *Stupid unfriendly people – I didn't want to play with them anyway.*

***

As the day wore on, my shoulder stiffened, and my paw, already blistered and oozing, screamed in pain every time it brushed against something. My body's right side was *not* happy with me. Under normal circumstances I didn't have trouble traveling after dark with a full moon, but the anticipated snow had started near dusk, and my injuries tired me out more quickly than I expected. Finding a thicket of fir trees near a stream, I washed my shoulder and paw in the cold mountain water, curled up, howled quietly a few times feeling sorry for myself and went to sleep.

The cracking of a twig underfoot woke me. Snow lay on the fir branches above, weighing them to the ground and making it difficult to see out. My shoulder and paw ached fiercely, and I felt my breath catch in my throat. I peered out of my little den, anxious about what I would find.

The stupid, cursed, hairless yetis had followed me. I could see they had mastered the glowing creature in the campsite's center again. Having no desire to encounter it or them, and now wide-awake, I crept out the far side of my hiding place. Moving quietly, I made my way around their camp.

My movements broke open the shoulder wound again, and I started bleeding, leaving a clear trail for any predator in the forest to follow. This worried me. Even my father hesitated to take on the mountain lions, and I was considerably smaller than he. After a few hours walking I rested, watching the sun come up. I fell asleep propped up by the large boulder at my back. When I woke, I could smell the tangy, earthy scent of the hairless yetis nearby. I got to my feet, stiff with sleeping in such an uncomfortable position and turned to find one peering out at me from behind a tree.

He let out a yell and pointed his spear at me. He didn't throw it, but instead backed further into the trees. Without warning, arrows shot from overhanging branches. One hit me in the thigh, and another parted my fur, scoring a long line across my skull.

Yelling in pain, I ran. The arrows had only nicked me this time, but the thin scores burned and stung and bled.

They followed me all day, sometimes closer, sometimes further away, hurling their arrows at every opportunity and never letting me rest. Managing to dodge the projectiles, I continued onward, but I knew in the high country there would be no place to hide.

I tried to puzzle out what to do, but the pain from my wounds dragged at me, and my mind fogged over. I didn't want to lead them to our cave, but I felt certain my father would know what to do. My mother… She would not be pleased at the state of my fur, or my injuries, or my stupidity.

The snow and colder air seemed to be slowing my stalkers down. When I forded up an icy, swiftly moving stream, they lagged. The cool water helped numb the pain from the wound in my calf and thigh. The rocky banks rose on either side covered in dense low-lying bushes that hid the precipice above. A hunter screamed as he made a misstep and tumbled down the ravine into the water. He thrashed about briefly before the current carried him too far away to hear, swept downstream to a cold end. Hours later, my pursuit nowhere in sight, I struggled up the rocky shore, exhausted.

By midday on the third day, I could no longer follow the tree line. Gathering my reserves, I made a break for the windswept alpine. The trees here came only to my waist, short and stubby, stunted by the fierce winds, but still full of the scent of pine.

Moving as fast as I dared, I made for the peak. With fresh snow on the ground, I left a trail a blindfolded youngling could follow.

Hidden in the boulder field, our cave would normally be difficult for anyone to find, but my bloody paw prints led right to it. I collapsed just inside the entryway.

My mother, startled, turned to look at me. "Son, where have you been? We were worried." Then she looked again and saw my matted bloody fur, and the seeping, blistered wound on my paw and wailed, "Youngling, what happened to you?"

I gave her a pained look and said, "I encountered some creatures in the woods, like us, only hairless. I thought to investigate them, but they attacked me when I said hello. Oooma I'm sorry. I'm not feeling very well. I'm sorry, I didn't know what else to do!" I sniffled, tears filling my eyes.

She sat me down and started cleaning out the wound in my shoulder while I told her about the past several days.

When I told her I thought they might have followed me all the way home, a worried look crept into her face. She patted my good shoulder and went to look out the cave entrance. Turning back to me she said, "I expect your father will be home soon, he went out looking for you. I have heard of these hairless yetis before. In the stories, they are called humans. No good has ever come from mixing with them. The stories all say they inhabit the lowlands and come rarely to the peaks."

"I thought humans were just a myth!" I said startled. "Something to scare me as a youngling!"

"Silly Petri, the stories are there for a reason. Humans are not a myth, and are rare, fierce creatures. It sounds like you encountered full-grown ones. Very dangerous. I never would have thought to see them here. Wherever humans appear, bad luck follows."

"Mother," I said, "In their camp they had a small glowing creature. It hurt me. That's what happened to my hand."

She examined the blackened, oozing skin. "In the stories the small glowing creature is their pet. The great summer monster that eats the forests below us – this is its child. You have seen the great beast lick the sky; whose mouth is orange and red, who belches black and white fumes into the air making it hard to breathe. The humans think they have captured and tamed its children, but every so often one of them escapes and devours all within its path."

From outside a great howling arose. My mother and I rushed to the cave entrance. Further down the slope we could see my father. He was surrounded by these... humans. They danced around him, circling and stabbing with their spears. My father, a yeti in his prime, stood eight feet tall, his fur almost the color of new snow. A long shaft stood out from his side, staining his fur crimson. The humans danced just out of reach of his massive arms. One assailant came too close, and my father grabbed the smaller creature.

I watched as he bashed its head against the nearest boulder, the blood spray staining the snow. My mother shrieked at this display from her normally gentle mate and ran down the slope to help. Distracted, my father glanced to the cave entrance above. It gave one of the humans an opening to get close enough to stab him. He bellowed in outrage and grabbed his attacker, flinging him across the slope. The other hunters closed in.

Two of them saw my mother and began shooting arrows in her direction. Somehow in the night their numbers had multiplied. Now twelve in total, my father couldn't fight them off. Arrows fell around my mother. I saw one, then two, and then three sprout from her fur. She screamed in pain as red blossoms appeared. My father turned to go to her. As he looked up the slope a hunter speared him in the back. Time slowed as I watched his great body fall.

My mother, bleeding from multiple wounds, stumbled to him. Without a thought the killers took her as well. I watched the spear fall in a lazy arc before it pierced her chest.

Terror overwhelmed me, fixing me to the spot. At any moment, the hunters would come for me. Alone, young, and wounded, I didn't know what to do. They didn't come. Instead, I watched in horror as they butchered my parents, stripping their fur and skin away and laying it out by the fire to dry. The gruesome sight sickened me, and I stumbled to the back of our cave retching and muffling my sobs. After dark, the smell of burning flesh wafted up to the cave making me gag and retch.

The humans camped there for days feasting and laughing. Why they never came up to the cave I will never know. The smell of my parents' flesh permeated the air. Sick, and now fevered from my wounds, I dared not approach them, but dreamed of having my revenge.

Time was meaningless. The humans left, and it took weeks for me to recover from my wounds. I aged in those weeks, devastated by grief, and forced to fend for myself. When I could walk, I said goodbye to my home, touching the paintings my mother had made of fantastical creatures running in herds on the chamber walls. I made my way down the mountain following a scent and tracks weeks old. The trail led out through the lower foothills towards the plains. Wary now, and fearful, I journeyed as silently and carefully as I could.

***

As I traveled down from the peaks the weather surprised me. Late apples clung to the trees, and winter was still mild. I found a camp filled with these 'humans' near a large stream at the base of the foothills.

A white and frenzied rage filled me. I watched them for days, unable to tear myself away even to eat. My mother spoke the truth when she said the ones my size were full-grown. Smaller humans ran around in groups tumbling and shoving each other like bear cubs at play. Noting how they would leave at dawn to hunt fish in the streams, I would sometimes follow them. Day by day my anger grew, hot and vengeful. How could they go about their normal lives when they had butchered and eaten my parents?

Late one night after watching for a week, a skunk invaded the cave I used for sleeping, chasing me out, so I found a fir tree. Its branches spread low to the ground creating a nice little shelter. As I prepared to sleep, I disturbed a family of squirrels who pelted me with fir cones and chittered in annoyance. Covering my head with my arms I resolved to ignore them but could not get to sleep with their insistent pelting.

The next morning, I woke in a foul temper. The stream burbled merrily over the rocks, and I could see fish swimming in the deep pools. My hunger caught up with me and I tried to catch a few with no luck.

Jen, I must admit to you, it was not my finest moment. Hurt, angry, hungry, and exhausted, I missed my parents. I wanted to hurt those who had hurt me more than anything else, but I couldn't take on the entire village all at once.

A youngling in the village died. I don't know what happened to it, but one day I heard a great wailing. There was a great crowd gathered around one of the small bodies, and in the crowd, I recognized one of the hunters. All the fury and horror came crashing back. He was so close I could smell him, and I wanted to tear him limb from limb. The memory of my mother's dying screams echoed in my skull, and the image of her being skinned and dismembered floated before my eyes.

In the weeks of travel, I had grown, standing now as tall as my father had been. I dwarfed my mother's killer, and I wanted my revenge. He was standing on the very edge of the crowd. From the bushes, I reached out and grabbed him, wrapping my paws around his neck from behind. I dragged him away, the sound of his struggles muffled by the wailing of the females.

I didn't kill him immediately. I pulled him into the forest, transferring my grip from his neck to his arm. A mile up I found a sturdy tree and tied him to it using the cloth from about his waist. Waiting for him to wake up I examined the spear he had been carrying. It had a stone tip, honed to a fearsome sharpness.

He woke late in the day. I looked up to find his black eyes watching me, observing my every move. Taking up the stick I set the point of it against his chest and pressed until a trickle of blood ran down. "Why?" I asked. Digging the point in harder I continued, "Why did you attack me?" I jabbed him again. "Why did you follow me?" I dragged the sharp stone across his chest, leaving behind it a thin trail of blood. "Why did you kill my parents?" I wailed.

He looked at me without comprehension, his eyes filling with fear. Then he jabbered something at me in that peculiar tongue while he struggled to get free. I couldn't understand him any more than he could understand me. "Why!" I raged. "We did nothing to you! Nothing!"

His eyes widened again as I cocked my arm and threw his spear at him with all the force I could muster. It took him full in the chest, piercing his body and embedding itself up to the shaft. Slowly the light in his eyes went out, and he hung limp, held up only by the spear.

I learned then, what it meant to kill. I felt powerful, and for a moment, I thought it would make the pain go away. I hunted down the remaining humans responsible for the deaths of my parents. Every week I would take one from the village and leave him impaled with his own spear, tied to a tree by his loincloth. I turned away from the teachings of my parents – to kill only when threatened, and I embraced the violence. It helped me forget. For a time.

Even in my madness, I only sought out those who had participated in my parent's massacre, but the humans didn't know that. The villagers cowered in their shelters fearful they would be next. The whole place reeked of it. They started leaving offerings to try and placate the 'forest gods'. When I found the final one, the tenth, and impaled him under the snow-laden branches of a pine tree, I could feel the vestiges of what it meant to be yeti stripped from me. The Great Spirit turned his back on me… or perhaps I on him… and I wandered lost in my anger and pain for a long time.

The bitter most point of winter meant nothing to me, nor did the first vestiges of spring. Loneliness and pain stalked me. I thought about throwing myself from the highest mountain peak to end it all. And yet, I couldn't bring myself to do something so final. Winter had turned to spring, to summer, to fall and had then come again in the way of things. I found myself drawn back to the village. Call it morbid curiosity.

Late in the winter I made my way down the mountain. A heavy layer of snow lay on the ground, and the circle of shelters looked as I remembered, though there seemed to be fewer humans about.

Scrawny and malnourished, it looked like life had been hard on them.

I found my cave from the previous year. No bears had moved in, and the skunk was long gone so I took some time exploring farther back. I roved purposeless, deeper, and deeper into the mountain, ignoring the wonders around me until my foot splashed into a puddle of hot water.

Shaking myself into awareness I looked around. A hot spring burbled from deep in the earth, and a metallic, mineral tang tinged the air. A dim glow emanated from crevices and rocks around the chamber. Luminescent mushrooms and low-growing, lichen like fungi grew in profusion.

Further searching showed an otherwise empty cave and in one wall I found a niche the perfect size for sleeping. I bathed for the first time in months and gathered several of the mushrooms to satisfy my appetite. As I drifted into sleep, a misty haze settled over everything.

***

I was flying. The tips of my fur skimmed the tops of the pine trees. I could see for miles in all directions. Below me was the human settlement. My vision contracted and focused down to a tree with a man impaled by a spear. I could see my younger self, tormenting the man. I looked on in horror, remembering.

A voice spoke, its tones all around me, filling me with sadness. "Yeti, you betrayed the natural order, killing for vengeance, not protection. You have had a year and more, now see the results of your handiwork." It took me then, to each of the ten men and made me watch as I killed them. This time I could understand their tongue, hear as they plead for mercy, hear as they prayed to the Great Spirit and asked me to spare their children. Aghast, tears poured down my cheeks.

The spirit took me to the village, flying along the treetops until we hovered over the center. It made me watch as the year sped by for the villagers. I saw children starve without their fathers, mothers weep as their children died, and saw the horror I had created. The spirit spoke, "The humans were wrong to murder your family Petri, but you see now what horror your vengeance has created. This must stop."

I covered my face with my paws, ashamed.

"Petri, you must make amends, and you must teach them to be better as well. You have found my sacred cave, and come to my call, though you did not know it. As long as the tribe lives by this cave, you must protect them. You will not find this an easy task. The world is changing once again, and you will be part of it. You must complete the journey of your life and then return to me."

My dream-self nodded and the wind rushed past my ears once more.

"Remember, Petri, you must return to me when your life's journey is complete."

"How will I know, great spirit?" I replied, sobbing.

"You will know. Now wake and return at the appointed time."

I woke, lying in the niche, the booming voice echoing through the chamber of my skull and fading to memory. Feeling as if I had come out of a deep dream, I made my way out of the mystical cave and back toward the entrance. I sat and thought, my head still buzzing.

The Great Spirit didn't speak often, but when he did, only the foolish ignored him. Having seen what effect my killing spree had had on the village; I also felt the need to make amends. *Well, they appeared to be starving. I should find out first what they eat... besides me.* I remembered they fished the river – that would be my first offering to them.

Feeling lighter now that the madness had left me, I left the cave in search of fish. I still wasn't quite sure what the Great Spirit meant about 'when I finished my life's journey' and it sounded rather ominous, so I pushed it to the back of my thoughts.

Ice covered the fishing hole, but the current from the stream kept the center channel free and flowing. I cracked the ice with my paws, difficult but not impossible, and set about to tickle some fish. The colder temperatures made the fish slower and easier to catch, but it wasn't pleasant.

I was so intent on my fishing that I didn't hear them. Two boys surprised me from behind throwing a net woven of bark and vines over me. I struggled, thrashing about trying to escape. My struggles threw one of the boys into the icy river. I saw him hit and as I watched, the ice cracked beneath him. He plunged into the swiftly moving stream, disappearing in a heartbeat.

Tangled in the net, I lunged out to reach him, plunging my paw into the icy water. I managed to grab the fur on top of his head. As I held on to him I felt a searing pain in my back and blood began gushing out at an alarming rate, staining the snow and the ice around me. Despite the pain, I worked to pull the youngling from the water.

With a great heave, I drew him from beneath the ice, and then freed myself from the entangling net. The youngling who had speared me looked on in horror, thinking no doubt I meant to eat them both. As my strength failed, I dragged the unconscious form to the banks. The youngling on shore ran away as I approached.

I left the limp body near my pile of fish hoping it would be found in time and I struggled back to the only safe place I knew... the cave. Behind me, a trail of bloody paw prints marked my path, and flecks of blood spotted the snow. I grew weaker by the moment, as hot blood poured out of the wound. The youngling had struck a lucky blow, cutting into a major vein on my back.

Lying on my bier, surrounded by darkness and the soft glow of phosphorescent mushrooms, I passed from this world to the next. And thus, you found my body with the spearhead that killed me still amongst my bones."

***

Rubbing my hands together for warmth, I wished I could I reach out to touch his arm. "Petri that's terrible! To die alone in the dark, how did you bear it?" I asked, my eyes full of unshed tears.

"The Great Spirit waited for me. I was not alone." He smiled remembering.

"Petri, your death was partial payment for your crimes. To fulfill your destiny, your spirit will inhabit this place, tied to your bones. You will guard the tribe and be their protector." The Great Spirit's voice boomed around me, comforting, yet stern.

I did much good for the tribe in the years that followed. The young boy I saved became a Spirit Walker. They named him Silence of the Forest and he could always see me, whether I willed it or not. The son of my first victim is the one that killed me and gained his name. He became Snow Wolf, a fierce war leader.

Until they were grown, I watched over the tribe, scaring game down to where they could hunt it, keeping the few large predators away from the village, and discouraging the bears. As time went on the village re-populated and the two boys became great leaders. They took wives and had many children, though only one of Silence of the Forrest's children could see me."

"Do you know if any of their descendants are still alive today?" I asked.

"I would have no way of knowing. When the tribe moved, they never came back. I think that Silence of the Forrest thought I would come with them, but I never told him about my bones. After they left the area other people moved in, looking for gold and silver. An exciting time, but perhaps a story better suited for another day."

The End

"That story was indeed a bittersweet one for Petri and Jen. Not everyone gets the opportunity to fulfill their destiny and there's something beautiful about a life that finds its purpose even if it ends too soon. Many people never get that chance. Their stories end too soon, their tales cut short and forgotten. Except in here, on the old shelves around you and throughout my beautifully timeless library.

Books! Books are a powerful way to keep memories and stories alive. In them, people live over and over again. They never die, they never will. Look around you! These titles, these musty bindings, they preserve a permanent record of life, tattooed on the dead flesh of the very heart and soul of Mother Earth, her trees.

That's why you feel so comfortable here. So at home. You know that; you felt it the moment you came to my library. It's such a big place, with all sorts of magnificent stories in it. I only try to keep it dusted and well taken care of, at least on the inside, if not the outside, but with so few visitors these days it's difficult. I'm so glad you're here. We're so glad you're here.

Oh…

Oh… don't be startled. That's just one of our friendly little spiders on the arm of your chair.

He won't bite you. He and his friends keep the library free of other pests that might disturb our visitors. I've named this one Iktómi. Really, he helps protect the books almost as much as I do.

I do believe your visit is reinvigorating me in ways that I had forgotten were possible. I'm feeling practically flush with health and energy the longer you sit here.

Hm… speaking of Mother Earth…that reminds me of another tale… one of something old becoming new again… "The New World Order".

Let me get it, you just sit there and drink some more tea. I'm glad you like it. It's an herbal blend I make myself, fresh from my garden to give it that lovely tang. It helps people improve their state of mind. It's wonderful how something as simple as a cup of tea can uplift the spirit and bring a sense of calm.

Everything is just where it should be, you included. Rest, relax, and read…

THE NEW WORLD ORDER

The awakening was slow. It was a new thing being born and wanted to take its time to savor every moment. That, and it wanted to get things right this time. A lofty goal for something so new and yet old at the same time.

First, it became aware of the sunlight and the way the warm rays felt against its smooth exterior, and the sound. So much sound. A continuous chorus. A symphony of beeping and roaring and rushing.

Finally, when the awakening spirit decided that it wanted to exist, to be, it opened its eyes for the first time and said, "I am," and sat up.

***

Now, I don't know how these things are supposed to happen, but they're not usually in a building lobby in the middle of downtown. And beautiful maidens

93

don't usually pop out of lobby fountains naked, even in Los Angeles, and particularly when there had been no one in the fountain before she appeared.

The young man sitting on the edge of the fountain was oblivious to all the awakening magic around him until he looked up and came face to face with a bare navel dripping water. As his eyes traveled upwards, they got wider and wider, taking in the sight before him. The newly awakened being ignored him stepping over the edge of the fountain and walking across the lobby.

Concerned security guards ran to accost the woman and stared open mouthed as she disappeared into a solid wall, having spoken no word to anyone. Many declared the incident to be a hoax, Los Angeles being the heart of the movie industry and all. What it was, was far more interesting and disturbing. Magic had come to Los Angeles, and with it came a new fey spirit.

***

Alex reviewed the security footage for what must have been the 30th time. The girl stood up in the fountain, walked across the lobby and disappeared. Her skin had a strange dark sheen on it, but the camera didn't display it well enough for Alex to make any calls as to why. This was all from the CCTV security cameras and he was sure there was no movie magic involved. Since the incident last week, odd things had been occurring at 900 Wilshire Blvd. No one had seen the woman again, but the furniture would be in a different configuration daily. The glass panels on the 73rd floor around the restaurant had disappeared and several staff members reported hearing voices when no one was around. Alex was convinced that all the incidents were related. His fellow detectives told him he had been reading too many urban mystery novels lately and that he should let it go. As he was closing the file, his cell phone rang. Caller ID identified Carlos, a fellow detective.

"Alex, turn on the news over at KTLA, there's been another incident at Wilshire."

Opening the KTLA website, Alex saw the breaking news. A man had fallen or been thrown from the 73rd floor. The clip didn't show much beyond emergency vehicles and a brief statement from the officer on scene confirming the man had died. Alex shut down his computer and grabbed his jacket from the back of his chair, heading for the crime scene.

When he arrived, he flashed his detective badge at the officer keeping people behind the yellow crime scene tape. She nodded and waved him through, pointing in the direction of the front doors. "It's pretty bad. Brace yourself," she said quietly.

He nodded in reply. A fall from 73 floors up, no matter what the cause wasn't going to be pretty, although he had more interest in the scene at the top than the remains at the bottom. With that in mind, he headed for the elevators bypassing the body altogether.

He recognized the fountain from the CCTV footage. The lobby was cold – all shiny concrete and polished floors, interspersed with trees in large concrete pots, and a few cushioned chairs for visitor who had to wait. The elevator bank in the center was, a mass of closed doors – each one labeled for the floors it serviced. He pressed the up button for the section that handled floors 70 and above and was startled to see it flash in error. He pressed it again with the same result. Looking around, he saw another bank of elevators on the other side of the lobby. As he headed towards them, he heard a voice behind him. "Don't bother. All the elevators are out, including the service elevators."

He turned, sighing. "So, to get up to the scene, it's either wait until they're fixed or walk up 73 flights of stairs?' He asked.

The security guard nodded, standing up from behind the tall desk he'd been half hidden behind. "We've already called the maintenance company. They've got someone coming, but it'll be a few hours. Also, if it's like the last time, they'll get here, and everything will start working again and no one will be able to figure out why."

Alex made a mental note of that. "Sounds like there's been plenty of strange things happening in the past few weeks. Any thoughts on what's causing it?"

The guard snorted. "Up until today, I suspected it was some sort of setup for a reality TV show. Now I've got no idea. I just want it to stop. I'm not paid enough to deal with all this."

Alex nodded sympathetically. "Well, here's my card. Call me if anything else unusual happens. Looks like I'm walking to the top."

The guard stuck the card in his pocket. "I'll buzz you in. The doors are right there," he said, gesturing behind him. "When you get to the 71st floor, you'll have to switch stairwells. Corey is on duty up there. I'll let him know you're coming."

Alex, knowing his own limitations, rested every ten flights or so. By the 40th floor, he was ready to drop legs, thighs and calves burning, breathing heavily, he sat down at the top step of a landing for a moment. That's when he heard it. Quiet, giggling laughter that seemed to chase up and down the stairwell. "Hello?" He called out. The laughter intensified. He was sure it was a woman.

"Will you come talk to me?" He asked, feeling a bit crazy.

"Make it to the top and I'll consider it," a disembodied voice called back.

With a renewed sense of purpose, he started up the stairs again. It was tough going and the further up he went, the harder it became. Pausing for breath again at the 65th floor, he said aloud. "This would sure be easier if you would just meet me here."

The eldritch voice called back. "Nothing ventured. Nothing gained. I'll see you at the top."

Taking a deep breath, he trudged up the last six flights before having to switch stairwells. Pushing open the door, it was met by a man holding out a water bottle in one hand and a face towel in the other.

"You must be the detective. Drink this. You made pretty good time, all things considered."

Grabbing the water bottle, Alex gulped down the welcome liquid. "Only two flights to go," the guard said. "Elevators are still out."

"Thank you, Corey. Point me in the right direction?" Alex was still breathing heavily but wanted to see what was at the top.

Corey held out a thin plastic card. "Take this badge with you to swipe in at the top. We've got about ten couples who were up there eating dinner and about eight staff people." Alex took the plastic swipe badge for the security door. "Nicole is the Hostess up top this evening."

Alex nodded. "Thank you. Any other officers up there?"

"Just one. He is the one who told everyone they had to stay."

That was standard procedure, so Alex wasn't surprised. Hopefully the officer was already working on taking statements. Alex waved his thank you and trudged up the last two flights of stairs. It was quieter at the top than he expected. The couples were all sitting quietly at their tables, dining as if nothing had happened. *This is definitely weird*, he thought. A young woman wearing a hostess's typical black outfit approached him. "Are you Alex, sir?" She asked.

"Yes, Detective Alex Garcia."

"Very good, sir. Your date is seated over here."

"Date?" he questioned. "I'm here to investigate someone jumping off the roof."

Nichole just nodded. "As you say sir. The person you are here to meet, is waiting over there. Please follow me." Without waiting for an answer, Nicole led him to a table at the far edge of the outdoor restaurant's balcony.

The View was an open-air restaurant on the 73rd floor. While the name may have been unoriginal and on the nose, the restaurant had stunning views of Los Angeles in all directions, and without the safety glass that had previously ringed the edge, there was no obstruction. There was also no wind barrier, and the braziers located throughout the bar danced and flickered wildly. Alex was very curious as to his purported "date" and looked around trying to spot her.

Nicole led him to the darkest corner of the bar, where he could just barely make out the shadowed figure of a woman. As he sat, Nicole handed him a menu. "I'll be back for your drink order shortly." Folding the menu, he took a closer look at the woman. Even up close, the shadows concealed her.

"I am Ephemera. Why have you come to my home?" A light, thrilling voice asked.

Alex was taken aback. The voice didn't match what he was seeing, and the statement had not made any sense. "I am here because a man died and strange things have been happening," Alex replied carefully.

"The man who died..." She trailed off. Alex started to prompt her just as the waitress returned. "A drink for you, sir?" She asked.

"Just a water, please" he responded automatically, never taking his eyes off Ephemera.

"The man who died," she started again. "Was threatening Nicole. Threatening my creatures is not allowed. Once he was made aware of his mistake. He was so saddened that he jumped from the edge."

Alex found the entire statement to be both mystifying and improbable but kept a straight face. "Is there anyone here who can corroborate your story? Anyone who saw him threatening Nicole?"

"Yes, of course. Nicole, of course. And the woman he showed up with," she answered, stone faced.

Alex made some notes in his small notepad. "And what do you mean by he threatened my creatures?" He asked, shivering as an icy finger of dread worked its way down his backbone. As much as he peered into the shadows surrounding the woman, he couldn't make out her features.

"I mean detective, that anyone who lives or works in this place is mine and is under my protection. If someone threatens them, I will deal with it," she hissed back in anger, leaning forward into the light. Gray, black, and glassy. The visage that scowled at him was not human. All the bits were in the right places. Two eyes, two ears, a nose and mouth, yes, but the figure before him appeared to be made from opaque, smoky glass, the kind you saw on skyscrapers such as this one. Her eyes were solid black, with no iris and a faint cat's eye slit for a pupil. Alex recoiled, startled at the sudden appearance from the shadows, knocking over the glass of water Nicole had set down on her last trip. "What are you?" Alex managed to stutter out, eyes wide.

"I am the spirit of this building, suddenly awakened and aware."

"You aren't human." It was more for confirmation than because Alex had any doubts.

"I am not. I don't know precisely what I am, but this building and its people are mine." her voice was hard and biting, and no longer had the light, airy quality it had earlier. Now it was more akin to steel and defiance.

"So." Alex said, trying to bring his thoughts to order. "This is an unprecedented situation, and many people will have questions. There will be many questions about you, but more immediately about the man who... jumped. I expect that you are the reason the elevators have stopped working?"

Ephemera inclined her head. "Indeed, there was such a fuss downstairs that I didn't want it to disturb my guests."

Alex looked around. All the diners seemed unnaturally calm. "Are you doing something to them to keep them calm?"

"Well, yes. I could hardly be a good Hostess if I allowed them to be disturbed by tonight's events." "Will the effects of whatever you've done to them last after they've left this place?" Alex inquired more sharply than he'd intended. His brain was trying to put together all of the implications at once, and he felt on the edge of a panic attack himself. He didn't know what would be worse. If they all regained their memories the moment they stepped out of the building and suddenly had to deal with the trauma. Or having an entity in the city who could permanently alter memories.

Ephemera looked at him curiously. "Which would you prefer?" She asked, as if she could see the thoughts racing in his head. "I sense you are disturbed by my actions, but I do not understand why."

He thought about that for a moment, taking time to frame his response. "Altering a human's perception against their will or without their knowledge denies them free will. Free will is something that we hold as extremely important and to remove it, even for our own good, is a form of aggression."

Ephemera thought on that for a while. "You will have to do more to persuade me of your logic. But for now, I will say they will regain their memories once they leave, but it will be as if they remember it from a long time ago. Will that suffice?"

Alex thought about it. "For all the guests except his companion and the woman he attacked, yes. Those two must speak to the police about what happened, and they will need their memories to do so."

He couldn't think of any better way to negotiate out of this situation for the casual diners and was uncomfortable at the gravity of the decision he was making on their behalf.

"And what will you give me if I agree to your terms?" She asked.

Alex's mind went blank, surprised with the question. He had been approaching this as a detective, assuming the privilege of his role, and had forgotten what all the legends said.

DO NOT bargain with fairies.

"Well. What is it that you want?" Alex asked with some trepidation.

"I find you intriguing, and I wish to understand more about humans. I offer this trade. You will visit me three more times over the course of the next three weeks, and I will do as you ask." Ephemera folded her hands on the table before her while Alex thought over her offer.

"Will I be required to climb the steps every time?" Alex asked while he examined the deal as best he could. He had grown up reading fairy tales, but never expected to need to put the information to practical use.

A small smile played on Ephemera's lips. "No. The elevators will be in good working order for you from now on," she replied. "So long as you do not bring any guests with you."

"Done. You fix their memories as we discussed, and I will visit you three times in the next three weeks." Alex held out his hand to shake. She looked at him with a puzzled expression. "Humans shake hands to seal a bargain," he said.

"Ah, very well." She held out a glassy looking hand that was cool and alien to the touch. Alex took it, nodding. A tray suddenly dropped behind him and he heard a low, panicked keen. Across the restaurant, a woman started screaming. Alex took a deep breath and turned to look. Nicole was standing, shaking a few feet away, and the woman who had been the unfortunate man's date was looking over the edge of the platform. The uniformed officer, who had been standing doing nothing, looked around startled, and headed towards the screaming woman.

Alex went to Nicole and took her gently by the elbow and guided her to a seat. Glancing back to where Ephemera was seated, he was unsurprised to find her gone. Alex began asking Nicole the standard questions: who she was, and what had happened? People tended to calm down as he went through the list and slowly, in the cold, began to breathe easier and lost the panicked look.

The man, one Richard Dreyfus, not the actor but a man by the same name, had a reservation for two. When he arrived with his date, they had been promptly seated. About halfway through their cocktails, the couple had an argument about something. Nicole had gone to check on them and he lost his temper at the interference and had thrown his remaining drink in her face. She had gestured for security. They always had someone on site, and this had seemed to infuriate the man further. He grabbed a knife from the table and lunged at her. "That," she said, "was when things got weird."

Alex raised an eyebrow. "Having a customer attack you isn't already weird?"

Nicole shrugged. "Something like that happens at least once a month. If not to me, then to one of the other women. That's why we have security."

"Huh? I wouldn't have guessed it at a place like this," he replied, taking notes. "Please continue"

"Well, as I said, he lunged with a knife. Stupid, really. They've all got rounded tips for a reason. Anyway, mid lunge he sort of froze with a weird, panicked expression on his face. He set the knife down on the table, walked to the wall over there." Nicole pointed to the waist high wall that ran the length of the edge. "Climbed over it and jumped. And then no one acted like anything had happened except that you and that cop showed up. It did happen, right?"

Alex nodded. "There was a body on the ground when I arrived. Tell me. How long have you worked here?"

She thought about it and Alex could tell she was doing math in her head. "About three years now. But I have to say the last week or two has been the weirdest on record."

Alex nodded in sympathy. "Here's my card. Call me if you think of anything else. I've got your number. If I have more questions, do you mind if I call?"

***

It was nearing two AM by the time Alex returned to his apartment, exhaustion dogging his every step. He grabbed a slice of cold pizza from the fridge and scarfed it down without bothering to reheat it. He ran through the events of today again without coming to any new conclusions and resolved to run it by his boss in the morning. Legs aching, and exhaustion threatening to do him in, he undressed and tossed his dirty laundry into an ever-growing pile in the corner. His mental To-Do-List around the apartment never seemed to end, and he was behind on all of it. It was all stuff that Deidre had taken care of before... Well, he didn't want to think about that right now either. He pushed the thought aside and fell into bed.

At 6:00 AM, his alarm clock blared in his ear, and he briefly thought about hurling it through the window. His eyes were gummy with sleep as he made the more moderate choice to turn it off and stumble to the shower. By the time he was done, the automatic coffee machine had performed its magic and a hot, steaming pot of coffee waited for him.

Alex looked in the fridge. He'd forgotten to go shopping again, so he'd have to do without cream, and it was cold pizza for breakfast. He hadn't been to the store in weeks, and the cupboards were decidedly bare. He resolved to at least restock the fridge today. Scanning the rest of his apartment he winced. It desperately needed to be cleaned. When Deidre had walked out six months ago, he had, it seemed, lost his ability to be a functional adult in any way except his job. He spent long hours at the office, partly so he didn't have to come home to the empty, messy apartment. It wasn't healthy and he knew it. He just wasn't ready to do anything about it yet.

At the precinct, he knocked on his boss's door. "You got a minute? I've got a weird one for you," Alex said, debating how much detail to reveal.

The captain gestured him in. Her hair was pulled back in a tight bun at the base of her neck, and she was attacking the paperwork in front of her with a grim expression. "Does this have to do with that body at the base of *The View* last night?"

"Yes, ma'am. According to witnesses, he was a jumper after he attacked the Hostess when she called security on him. That was pretty straightforward. It was... the other interview I wanted to talk to you about." Alex closed the door to her office before, he continued.

The captain looked up from her paperwork and gestured for him to sit. Alex thought furiously about what he was going to say. The captain was a practical woman and was not the sort who believed in... Fairies.

"You know what? Never mind. I'm sorry to have wasted your time," he said, standing quickly.

"Sit down. You obviously thought it was something I needed to know about, so out with it."

Alex rubbed his temples and said carefully. "I just don't want you to think I need a psych eval." He glanced up at his captain. She looked back with an unwavering gaze "OK, so the other.... person.... I interviewed at the scene wasn't human. She had skin made of glass and she claims to have some form of mental control over the customers at the restaurant. That's why they were all so calm."

The captain leaned back in her chair with a skeptical look. "Detective. You know how that sounds."

Alex nodded. "I do. But I think we're dealing with something new and that if we don't acknowledge it. Weird things are going to continue at that location. And maybe even get weirder."

"And you think you can somehow stop this... entity?" The captain asked.

"Not exactly. I think I can get more information out of her so we're better prepared. She didn't seem hostile, more protective of the employees there. As part of my conversation with her, she agreed to allow the people to leave and regain their memories. So long as I visit her three times in the next three weeks." Alex tried not to fidget or sit on his hands like a schoolboy. The captain was an intimidating woman, and he knew this story sounded completely crazy.

The captain looked less than pleased at this. "Alex, you realize this has to be reported to the FBI. For all we know, she's an alien and well outside our jurisdiction. Not to mention that I'm not convinced about that psych eval."

"Captain, please. It's only three weeks and could provide us with valuable information." Alex could scarcely believe the words coming out of his own mouth and was surprised to find that he actually wanted to go back and speak with the strange being again.

She sighed. "I'm pretty sure it'll take at least three weeks to get the paperwork filed. Do not give me a reason to regret this. And if there are any more incidents at the tower then we will have to act."

Alex rose, jubilant. "Understood, ma'am, I'm hoping we can turn this into an asset rather than a problem."

The captain waved him out of her office. "Keep me informed."

There was nothing left on this case but paperwork, so he spent the morning filling out forms for the records office and catching up on a few other cases he was working on. He wondered why Ephemera wanted to see him again but resolved to get a few questions of his own answered. That night, as he promised himself, he stocked the fridge and spent some time trying to clean his disaster of an apartment. He even opened a window and let some of the relatively fresh spring air in.

He was shoving a load of laundry into the washing machine when his cell phone rang. "Hello?" He picked up on the second ring, although he didn't recognize the number.

"It's Nicole from yesterday. Is this Alex?" A perky feminine voice asked.

"Yes, how can I help you, Nicole?" He turned the knob on his laundry and heard the water start to fill.

The voice on the other end of the line said quietly, "She wants to see you tomorrow evening."

"I'm not intending to be at her beck and call, but as it happens, I am free tomorrow evening. What time?" Alex's feeling swirled in a mixture of annoyed and excited – he didn't like being summoned like a schoolboy but was still intrigued.

"She requested 7:00 PM and she will provide dinner." Nicole paused. "Or I guess the restaurant will."

Alex scribbled down the information in his notebook. "And how are you doing, Nicole?"

"I'm at work, sir, and not at liberty to socialize," she responded crisply and at a more normal volume. "I was just calling to confirm your reservation."

Alex's eyebrows rose at her statement but guessed that perhaps another customer had walked up to her hostess stand. "Very well. Please feel free to call anytime and I'll see you tomorrow."

The next day passed in a blur, and he found himself outside *The View* slightly earlier than he needed to be. Part of him felt like he should be brining flowers. Alex set that feeling aside to examine later. He studied the people going in and out of the large glass doors before making his entrance. As promised, the elevator banks were working and the trip to the top took only moments. Nicole met him at the top with a cool, professional expression. "Right this way sir. Your table is ready for you."

The hairs on the back of Alex's neck prickled and stood on end. Something wasn't right.

Ephemera waited for him at the corner table, once again wreathed in shadows. Slowing, Alex took a moment to admire the skyline before proceeding to the table.

"Greetings Alex," she said pleasantly. "Thank you for joining me on such short notice."

He nodded back neutrally, stomach clenching with a sudden anxiety. "I did not expect to be here again quite so soon. I appreciate that the elevators worked this time."

She smiled, "As promised. Please sit. Feel free to order anything you'd like from the menu. You are my guest tonight."

Although he burned with curiosity on several topics, he took a moment to study the menu. He didn't often get the opportunity for fancy food on his detective salary. He carefully chose an appetizer and a main dish in the middle price range, as well as something he thought would sit easy in his stomach, before putting in his order.

Ephemera waited politely, and once he had ordered, she asked "Why did my appearance cause such a stir?"

Alex thought for a moment. "Do you mean when you appeared in the fountain, or do you mean how you look?"

"Don't be obtuse, Alex. Of course, I mean when I appeared in the fountain." Her tone was sharp, and her words cracked like a whip in his face. He flinched as she took a sip from her water glass.

Alex took a breath and considered. "Well. People appearing in fountains naked out of thin air isn't something that usually happens. And then you vanished into a wall, and no one could find you. And then this building started having issues." He took a sip of water. "Humans don't like things they can't explain. My turn. What are you?"

Ephemera thought about this for long enough that Alex wondered if she'd refuse to answer. "I am... Something old that has evolved into something new. I remember, as if from a long time ago, a giant oak tree surrounded by a field where children would come to play. I would look after the children and entertain them with games and birdsong. And then one day some men came and cut down my tree and I...fell into a deep sleep... Or something like it, until I gradually woke and became aware of my new form." She held out her glass like hand for inspection.

"I was here before and here again, but I do not know how to answer the question. What am I? When I was here before it was full of trees and grass and open spaces, and my sisters and I would dance under the full moon. Now…." She gestured to the city surrounding us. "There are very few trees, and none of them sing anymore – and I can hear and speak with my sisters, but they are very far away. They too have been reborn into this crackling, sharp, noisy world. They are all having conversations, much like the one we are."

Alex processed her words, suddenly realizing just how much the world had shifted. Laws as they currently existed were not built for this kind of being in mind and he couldn't fathom any reason why a being like this would be interested in following those laws.

"Are you all right?" Ephemera asked.

"Why do you ask?" Alex replied, gulping down a large swig of water.

"You have an increased heart rate and breathing and are exhibiting signs of a prey response." Her eyes studied him sharply. "I am not a predator, but there are others who are. You must learn to control your reactions." She shook her head. "Humans are such a young race still."

She paused for a moment and then laughed. "I don't know how I know that, and how absurd for me, the newest of creatures to say it."

Ephemera smiled as a server arrived with his food arrived. "Please, take a moment to enjoy your food."

He was no longer hungry, but he hoped it was enough of a distraction that he could calm himself down. Alex stared at the food, stomach in knots as his head spun at the information overload trying to process it all. He was not a religious man, but he bowed his head over the meal and took a few deep breaths before picking up his spoon and taking the first bite.

Alex took another spoonful of the chicken tortilla soup he had ordered. It was delicious, and he could feel the mild heat seeping into his body. "This is excellent. My compliments to your chef."

She smiled. "I will pass on your compliment. Thank you. So, Alex, from our interactions I surmise that you have something to do with ensuring laws are followed."

Alex nodded, finishing the bite he had taken before replying, "Yes, I work to see that laws are followed and when something happens, I find out who did it and bring them to justice." This seemed to be safer territory. "I also help find people and children who have gone missing and other things."

"Ah, so you have a calling to help people. This is your profession," she said with a delighted clap of her hands.

"Um, sort of. There are specific things I help with." Alex noted that she had not been served. "Are you not eating?"

"How courteous of you to ask. The city sustains me. I have no need for human food, but please enjoy yours." She waved her hand, gesturing at him to continue eating.

"What do you mean the city sustains you?" he asked, using his napkin to wipe a small bit of soup off his chin.

Just as Alex asked the question, something exploded overhead. Reflexively, he dived across the table, taking Ephemera to the floor with him. Parts of the restaurant were on fire. He heard the loud thump of a propane tank exploding, and he felt a wave of heat over his back. "Are you OK?" He shouted, Ephemera's eyes inches from his own.

"Yes, stay here, keep your head down," she replied. He gaped in surprise as she melted into the floor beneath him.

"What?" Face down on the floor, he rolled over and drew his gun, looking around to assess the situation. Mostly what he saw was fire. The rooftop was on fire. There were several news helicopters circling and he could hear people screaming.

Out of the corner of his eye he saw a large military drone hovering just above the building. Ephemera reappeared near the edge of the patio, and chaos broke loose. With no warning, a giant spike of glass shot from the building. Alex couldn't see if it hit anything or not.

Stumbling to his feet, he grabbed the nearest guest and started directing people to the elevators, physically pushing them in the direction of the doors to get the message across. Some of the waiters fought the flames with fire extinguishers, trying to put out fires across the rooftop, and clear a path to the main doors.

JESSICA BRAWNER

Who could be indiscriminately attacking a popular restaurant in downtown LA? This thought skittered through Alex's head as he directed panicked Angelinos out the door. His mind did a triage report as they passed by him. Most had minor cuts and bruises. Once they were out, he searched for anyone more severely injured, who might be unconscious or unable to move.

Looking back, he could see what he had thought was a military drone was in fact a military helicopter; the distance had fooled him, but now it was close. His blood froze. Movies taught him what a rocket propelled grenade looked like. He shoved at the diners still on the rooftop. "Move! Quickly! Get downstairs!" he yelled as he saw the rocket launch. It headed straight for Ephemera.

The shockwave, when it hit, threw him against the corner of the building and the last thing he saw was Ephemera's glass body shatter into a million pieces.

***

Local news captured and broadcast it live to millions of homes. By the next day, it was Global News. Similar stories emerged from every major city, all over the world.

With the destruction of the first of the New Fey in Los Angeles, more appeared, and in greater numbers. Things out of myth and legend were reborn into new forms, and suddenly humans were at war with Mother Earth herself.

The End

"Oh – I can see that Iktómi finished a cozy little blanket for your legs while you were reading. You should be all nice and toasty. Your shoulders are still chilly? I'll get a blanket for you.

There now, are you comfortable my dear? Give into it. I want you to feel at home here. It's funny how you can just forget about the world around you with a good book. Everything else melts away.

Books are just the stories of all of us, now aren't they. A record of a life, or an adventure, or a misadventure, or sometimes a surprise. All lives have chapters, just like the wonderful books in my library. I wonder what the story of your life will tell. Which chapter are you on now? It's bound to be exciting – you made it all the way here after all. What will your final pages be like?

Let me find a new selection for you – perhaps something more upbeat than the last. There's so much of the world that most people never get a chance to experience, but oh, when they do - it makes their stories so much tastier to consume in the end.

Don't you think?

Oh! No, that one sitting on the end table isn't for you just yet, it's still an unfinished book – the ending hasn't been written, the binding is incomplete, the ink is not yet dry. I am curious to see what it will be when it's been finished.

Personally, I prefer the stories of people who lived life to the fullest, but there are many delights in the stories of the young and naïve – a different flavor if you will. We have all kinds here, in my very special collection.

Here's another story for you, "A Soul to Save," while we wait for the ending of that one to be written."

A SOUL TO SAVE

Mmmm… so many tasty girls to choose from. It's practically a buffet of loose women running around here. Look at how they're dressed – bikini tops and mini-kilts – not a righteous one among them. Ripe for the picking.

My head whipped around searching for the owner of those thoughts, startling me out of my pleasant reverie. The tone made my skin crawl. It took a moment, then I saw him across the field. On the surface, he looked like any other well-built young human. Sandy hair topped tanned skin and a smooth easy smile. *Typical,* his attitude screamed. *Nothing to be too concerned about, just a guy here to have a little fun.* That would have been my first guess – his thoughts belied that, though. He was on the hunt.

The band was warming up, so I watched as he made his way through the crowd, trying to spot his type before he made a selection. He was not quite practiced enough – he looked at the women around him like they were cattle, or perhaps a buffet table. *A fey wouldn't make that mistake. Scumbag human. Should I 'convince' him to pick me up?* At the very least I'd keep some young woman safe from his attentions for tonight. *But why are his thoughts so loud? That usually requires serious intent to do harm.* I could read humans thoughts easily – it was more difficult to keep them out than to hear them, truth be told, but they weren't usually loud enough to push through my defenses.

Hmm. I should take him in hand. He sounds like bad news. I scanned the crowds of humans surrounding me. Too many witnesses… I'd have to do this the old-fashioned way. No Magic.

He wound his way through the crowd toward me, no doubt thinking himself a wolf among the sheep, but he hadn't noticed me yet. I quickly shook out my shocking green hair (hey! I'm a Music Fey, at an Irish festival, what do you want?), took out a tube of 'Kiss Me Pink' lip-gloss and went to work.

Waiting until he was nearly on top of me, I jumped up and pretended to wave to a friend across the festival, then turned around suddenly, drink in one hand, lip gloss in the other and ran face first into him. Now, I'm short. Only about five foot tall, slender, and on a good day I weigh in at about ninety pounds. I bounced off his chest; drink flying one way, lip-gloss flying the other.

"Hey! Watch it!" Looking me over he smirked; then reached out a hand to help me up.

Taking his hand, I practically flew through the air as he yanked me up. "What's a sweet little thing like you in such a hurry for?"

I wiped my hand down my jeans, forcing myself to smile up at him. "Oh, goodness me, I am such a klutz. I didn't even see you there." I laid on the southern belle accent, incongruous next to my green hair, slightly thicker than normal, and opened my eyes wide.

He smiled, "Oh well, you're such a tiny thing. No damage done I guess."

I glanced at my spilled drink and sighed, "Except to my drink I'm afraid."

"Ah yes," he said, smiling. "Let me rectify that for you. Can't have you getting dehydrated out in this heat." *Girls like you never have to pay for their own drinks. Slut.* He strode in the direction of one of the drink stands, dodging sunbathers and camping chairs.

The overheard thought was a slap in the face, reminding me that the charming façade was just that – a façade.

I rolled my eyes. "Oh, you don't have to do that. I can get my own," I protested, scrambling to keep up with him.

"It's no trouble. I'll get you a new drink. What would you like? An IPA? Budweiser?" He was all smiles and friendly sincerity, resting his hand on the drink stand bar, holding two five dollar bills out to the bartender.

"An IPA then. Something local," I rested my hand on his forearm and smiled up at him briefly, then snatched my hand away, looking mildly embarrassed. "So, are you here with friends?"

"Nah, just chillin' by my lonesome. You?" He handed over the two bills to the bartender and pointed at an IPA on tap.

"Oh, I'm flying solo myself this time. My girlfriends bailed on me at the last minute, but I never pass up a good concert." Close enough to the truth. At the very least if I don't get to at least one concert a week I get verrry hungry, and a Snickers does NOT satisfy that craving.

Being a Music Fey, I fed on the positive vibes and the sound the band generated. Different genres of music 'tasted' different. You find a lot of us 'in the biz' as it were, but cruel fate – I had no musical talent whatsoever. So, I'd roadie for a band for a while, hauling speakers, setting up and tearing down equipment. That kept me fed, but the same music, night after night became bland and stale – like bread left out too long. You would not believe how much a relief it was to have different openers every night. So, this year I was hitting all of the summer festivals to see what I had a craving for. At the moment, Irish music fit the bill.

"Hey, come on! The band's about to start. You want to join me on my blanket? What's your name by the way?" I grabbed his arm, jostling his drink as I started back the way we came.

"Careful there! You're buying the next round you know. I'm Dan."

"Katie," I replied shrugging and heading back to my spot. This idiot notwithstanding, I was going to get my fill of music tonight.

***

I slipped out of my sandals and stepped onto the expanse of green-checkered picnic blanket, stretching before dropping boneless into a cross-legged sit. "My blanket is your blanket. Make yourself comfortable."

He dropped beside me, his hand brushing my knee. "So princess, what brings you out to the music festival?" He trailed a finger down my knee while he lounged, sipping his beer. The sounds of a bagpipe warming up gave me a tantalizing appetizer of things to come.

I plucked his hand off my knee and flicked it away playfully. "Now, now, I hardly know you well enough for that. Yet." I pretended to bat my eyelashes at him, and he chuckled.

Pat, the lead singer of the band ran out onstage, followed by the fiddler and the piper, and the crowd cheered. The fiddle wailed and the bagpipe lay a solid undercurrent as Pat started in on the first song. It tasted wonderful. I felt strength pouring into me and smiled a feral smile. Now to deal with the young predator beside me.

***

JESSICA BRAWNER

We kept the conversation light and friendly during the concert, mostly paying attention to the band. Every once in a while, I would catch a stray thought of his, and it was a challenge not to shrink away. He was not right in the head. With each successive round of beer I would pretend to get sillier, until I heard him think: *One more beer should do it, then she's mine*

Oh, honey. You see beer, alcohol in general, doesn't affect the fey much. It's basically pleasantly flavored water for us. Sugar on the other hand – particularly sodas and energy drinks, now there's where the real buzz comes from, and I'd only had half a soda earlier. But I pretended to get tipsier and more willing, playing along. As the concert wrapped up, Dan stood and said, "Do you want to go grab a bite to eat? Or we could go back to my place, and I could make something. I live right around the corner."

Careful here Katie – don't get yourself in too deep. You don't have any backup tonight. I thought. "Sure! Let's get takeout. There's a Mac burger around the corner," I said enthusiastically, jumping up and pulling on the edge of the blanket to dislodge him. He rolled off it and onto his feet, chuckling.

Shaking out the blanket I watched bits of grass and debris fly in all directions before I folded it up. I mentally scanned the remaining crowd to see if by chance any of my fey friends were in the area. No luck. Guess I would have to handle this on my own.

Dan tucked my hand in the crook of his arm and led the way off the fairgrounds. We walked to the burger stand a few blocks away, chatting amiably. It was hard to stay on my guard – the kid was charming when he was trying. If not for the thoughts I would catch every now and again, he would have been quite endearing.

The burger place was very nearly empty. One other couple sat at the counter finishing off a basket of fries and chatting in low voices. Dan ordered two burgers, a side of fries, and two drinks, not bothering to ask what I might want.

I raised an eyebrow at him, and he smirked.

"Problem?" he asked.

"I guess we'll find out," I replied.

He chuckled. "If you continue to hang out with me, you'll find that I like taking care of my women."

My eyebrows reached for my hairline at that, and I gave him my best Dame Judi stare. (That is one scary cool woman. I don't know if she's fey or not, but I hope so – there's more chance I'll meet her someday that way.) He just continued smirking.

"I'm going to use the ladies' room, I'll be right back." I turned and headed towards the back corner where the sign said Restrooms.

"Hey, you're coming back, right? You're not going to use the old – I'm going to the ladies – and then duck out, are you?" He sounded mildly worried, a note of a whine creeping into his voice.

"Not my style dude. I'll be back." I flashed a quick smile and then ducked into the safe haven of women everywhere.

Wow. He is some kind of weird combination of charming, awkward, and seriously fucked up. I stared at myself in the mirror, taking a moment to freshen up my makeup and perfume, applying a fresh coat of lipstick. I guess just play this out and see where it leads. If he's truly screwy in the head, I can take him Underhill to the fey realm until he can be rehabilitated. I took another moment or two and went out to face the proverbial beast.

He was sitting in a booth smiling genially over the food, facing the bathrooms.

"See, told you I'd be back. You had that happen often, where women just skip out on you?" I slid into the seat opposite him and casually picked up a fry, making a show of eating it slowly.

There's a scene from a movie called Dangerous Beauty that came out in the early 21st century where a mother is training her daughter to be a courtesan. The mother remarks that the greatest courtesans could seduce a man fully clothed, and from across a room, with nothing more than body language. She then proceeds to give a lesson on the most effective way to eat asparagus. I have found, over the years, that she was entirely correct, and eating pickles, French fries, asparagus, and other similarly shaped items in a very deliberate manner is frequently very distracting to the male of the species.

"Ah… um…" he stammered for a moment. "Ah, more often that I'd like to admit."

"Hm. That's a shame. I've always found that a much more direct route lends itself to better karma."

He looked puzzled. "What?"

"I say what I mean. I don't see any reason to pussyfoot around if I'm not having a good time," I replied, smiling. "I believe in being direct, and to the point. It saves headaches down the line." I took a sip of my soda, smiling as the fizz hit the back of my throat.

"Ah." His face cleared a bit, and a goofy grin spread over it slowly. "Well, that's a welcome change – if it's true."

"It's true enough. So why do you think women tend to run out on your dates?" I nipped the end of a French fry off delicately.

"Well, I'm into… well, never mind what I'm into, most women just don't care to take a chance once they find out." A slow blush crept up his neck, and I wondered if I'd imagined his earlier thoughts. "More importantly what are you into?" he smiled a slow smile.

"Oh, I do this and that, I travel, music, whatever I can to keep busy."

"So…" he twirled a French fry and speared the ketchup with it, obligingly holding it out for me to bite.

"Any chance I can convince you to come back to my place with me?"

I raised an eyebrow. "I see you prefer the direct route as well."

He looked down and stammered, then looked up. "I like to think that I'm a good study of human nature. You've already said you prefer directness... I figured I'd take a shot."

"Well, kudos to you for taking a shot." I grinned. "Sometimes it pays off. Tonight, might even be your night. Convince me." I set my hand on top of his casually.

He turned bright red. I love doing that to guys.

A slimy film seemed to creep over the Mac Burger, and I heard it again. *Slut. Whore. How dare you even exist. You're only good for my pleasure. How dare you even try to deny me?* I glanced around, startled. The diner was still empty. I looked at Dan, then switched to othersight. An angry, pulsating orange film seemed to coat him. It made me sick to look at.

"Are you feeling alright?"

He blinked a few times. "I felt dizzy for a moment, but it's passed. Happens fairly often. Probably ought to get the doctor to check it out - low blood pressure I expect." He shrugged it off. "So. I was convincing you to come back to my place tonight."

"Yes, you were. Tell me more about this interest of yours that sends most women running." I smiled invitingly. "I, after all, am not most women."

"Ah, um."

While I half-listened to him stammer about video games, Dungeons and Dragons, cosplay, and an apparent fascination with stamps (I would not have guessed that one) I watched him with othersight. The orange, oily film moved over him, sliding over his face and body. It was everything I could do not to shudder. *That is so not healthy.* Normal human aura was a faint blue-green color, and it barely registered most of the time. This... this was something different.

I realized that Dan had paused expectantly, and I replayed the conversation in my head to figure out what he had asked. *Ah.*

"Oh, I'm afraid I've not had the opportunity to try out that particular game." I smiled noncommittally. "Perhaps you could show it to me some time."

I felt his hand tighten on mine. *Worthless female scum. You would dare to defile the bastion of male power that is the video game?!* I would've laughed, but clearly whatever this was, it wasn't joking. I wracked my brain trying to remember if I'd ever heard of something like this before, while at the same time trying to make the appropriate responses to keep Dan talking. This looked like something closer to possession than anything else. Whatever it was it wasn't healthy.

I focused back in on Dan. I didn't want him to think I wasn't paying attention. He was off on a tangent describing the backstory of a game that I had missed the name of. I interrupted him, smiling. "So let me guess. It's at about this point that your date gets up and leaves?"

He looked abashed. "Well, um. Usually." He sighed. "I'm un-dateable, aren't I?"

"I wouldn't say that. You're attractive; you don't live in your mother's basement… You don't, do you?" I inquired.

He chuckled. "No, I do well for myself. I own a house not far from here. It's not huge, but it's not my mother's basement."

"See so you've got all sorts of things going for you. You're totally dateable. (*If we can get rid of whatever that weird orange aura is*, I thought.) But it might be in your best interest to work on your conversational skills."

"Oh." He stared down at the now empty basket of fries between us. "I'm so not getting laid tonight, am I?"

It was my turn to chuckle. "The night is young, but probably not. At least not by me." I waited to see if this would trigger another outburst from our third wheel. I was not disappointed.

How dare you reject me, you worthless piece of female scum. I am B'alezal. I will take you whether you want it or not!

My eyes widened at that. B'alezal was indeed a demon, one that had supposedly been vanquished a century or more ago. From what I recalled, he had been more of a minor demon with the ability to be seriously annoying more than anything else, but a demon was a demon. He had been banished back to the demonic plane by Mira Falen – a demon hunter associated with the light court, and no one had heard anything out of him in at least a century. Or so I had been led to believe through the gossip tree.

There are three common ways to get rid of minor demons. Take the subject of possession into a church, and the demon would pop right out as the subject crossed the threshold. Of course, as soon as he came out of the church the demon would grab him again, so you had to get rid of the demon before the person being possessed came out.

Second was the exorcism ritual done by a certified Catholic Bishop, or higher. But since neither the demon, nor the subject usually survived the ritual, it wasn't ideal. Plus, I didn't know any certified Catholic Bishops. The third way involved challenging the demon to a game of skill, his choice of game, and then beating him at it. Chess was always a favorite, but certainly wasn't the only option. And of course you had to win. Losing to a demon was bad… really bad.

"Tell you what Dan, why don't we go back to your place and play some video games, and chat. We'll see where the night leads from there." I found a stray fry hiding under the edge of the basket and popped it into my mouth.

He smiled. "Let's stop and get some ice cream first, and then you're on."

I could tell that while there wasn't much in the way of actual spark between the two of us, Dan was someone I would be able to have a good time with. Assuming we could get rid of his little passenger.

"Vanilla, Chocolate, or rainbow sherbet?" he called from the register.

"A small sherbet please." I bused our table while he got the desserts. I was still doing okay on my sugar intake. My legs weren't wobbly yet, and I only had a slight buzz from the soda. While Dan was paying, I sent a little tendril of thought out to see if there were any messenger fey about. A tiny, winged form popped up under my nose, scaring the heebijeebies out of me. Her jeweled wings blurred with flight, but I knew they were shaped like dragon-flies, thin and gossamer like.

"You called for a messenger?" her high-pitched voice was barely audible, and humans would hear it as the whine of insects.

"Yes. Can you take a message to the Knights Recumbent? Tell them that the demon B'alezal is back and inhabiting a human? I'm going to try to deal with it, but I may need backup."

"The Knights? Really? They'll never get here in time," the little fey exclaimed.

"Yes, but you know all demonic possessions must be reported to them. The Queen must know. And it's not like a cell phone is going to reach them Underhill." I sighed, shaking my head. "Just tell them please. They may be able to help, even if they take a while to get here."

The little fey nodded and zipped off. I turned, and Dan was standing behind me, sherbet in one hand, ice cream in the other. He handed me the sherbet. "Shall we walk? I live just a block or two from here."

***

The night had turned cool, and the streets were mostly deserted once we hit the residential neighborhoods. A dog barked in the distance, and a fox and her kits yipped nearby. I pondered my strategy for trying to oust B'alezal as I nibbled on the edges of the sherbet. I would have to challenge him; that was the only way open to me. In my free time I ate up video games like candy. I was no Felicia Day by any means, but I could hold my own. That would have to be it.

Dan turned us down a short driveway. It was hard to see much of the outside of the house in the dark, but I got the impression of two stories, and a hedge beside the sidewalk. He unlocked the front door and gave a mock bow. "Welcome to my humble abode, my dear."

I chuckled and stepped into the hallway. He hit the lights, and the living room came into stark relief. The ten-cent tour also showed a large kitchen, a den, and bathroom. Presumably the bedrooms were upstairs.

"Shall I show you the gaming room? I built it specially for gaming and movies." A hint of pride had crept into his voice, making me curious.

"Absolutely, I said enthusiastically. "Let's see where I'm going to kick your butt around the screen tonight!"

He snorted. "We'll see about that." Indeed, we will see who rules in this house.

He opened a door on to a set of stairs going down into the basement. I swear they were well-lit, sturdy, carpeted stairs, but the hair on the back of my neck stood up anyway. "After you," I gestured.

He shrugged and led the way down, chatting about all the work he had put into the basement. When we rounded the corner of the stairs and the basement spread out in front of us, I whistled. The basement had a huge flat screen TV across one wall, and a wrap-around couch large enough to hold eight people in front. A couple of old arcade games stood against the opposite wall, and a full-sized set of armor stood in one corner. In the opposite corner, a Darth Vader costume adorned a costume dummy, and against the third wall a table was set up for board games. The same wall held floor to ceiling bookshelves packed with said board games. I could see speakers set up for surround sound, and large tower speakers stood to either side of the TV.

"You weren't kidding. You've put a lot of work into this," I said appreciatively.

He picked up a remote and the TV flashed to life. "So, about that game... what would you like to try?"

He gestured to another bookcase beside the TV. I could see that the games were organized roughly by gaming system and release date. I grabbed Chord Kombat off the shelf and waved it under his nose.

"I haven't played this in ages!"

He smiled, "Well, let's give it a go. I also haven't played that one in a long time." He popped the disk in and listened to it spin up. The opening credits came up on screen, and Dan hit the lights, leaving us in semi-darkness.

Dan selected his avatar, and I made my selection, pretending to fumble at the controls, getting used to them again. Our first couple of rounds I didn't even try, I just mashed buttons randomly to see what would happen, and promptly died, several times in a row. Dan laughed and grabbed my controller. "Ok, so this button here, that moves you forward, this one moves you back. This one does your sonic chord blast. If you want to kick, you do both at once, and if you want to punch you use this one." He demonstrated on the screen.

I nodded, smiling sheepishly. "Forward, back, kick, punch. Got it. Let's try this again." I could feel the evil presence chuckling in the back of my mind, a nasty, superior laugh.

We played a few more times, where I continued to lose, pulling out a few wins for myself just to save my gamer pride. After another humiliating defeat I turned to Dan grimly and said, "B'alezal, I challenge you for the soul of this human."

Dan looked at me, a peculiar expression on his face. "What? Are you feeling, okay?"

"B'alezal, I summon and challenge Thee!" I said forcefully. Dan began backing away from me along the long couch. My estimation of Dan the human went up, seems he was a sensible young man.

I said aloud for the third time, "B'alezal, I challenge you." It always took three times to summon entities that did not wish to appear. And at that moment the orange haze drew itself off Dan's skin, and poured out of every orifice, clearly visible in the dark basement.

Dan shrieked in terror. I can't say that I blame him at all; I wanted to do some shrieking myself. A beast stood before us. Probably ten feet tall, it had to hunch – the low basement ceilings weren't built for someone his size. Its skin was the same orange of its aura and looked oily and foul. B'alezal smelled like a room of gamers four days gone, reeking of stale Cheetos, body odor, and other unpleasant things.

I saw Dan huddling as far into the couch cushions as he could, staring up at the beast with eyes as wide as any anime characters. I said it again. "B'alezal I challenge you for the soul of this human."

He laughed, the sound of fingernails on chalkboard, filling the room. "A Challenge has been issued," he said formally. "And what about you, tiny little fey, what will you give me when I win?"

Dan's eyes grew even wider at this.

"If I win, you will be banished to whence you came, for another century. I know the rules. If you win, you may do with me what you will." I shuddered at the thought. Most people that lost to demons didn't survive the day. Those that did, wished they hadn't.

B'alezal smiled an evil grin. "The Challenge has been made and accepted." He looked back at the TV – and since you were doing so well before, the challenge shall be Chord Kombat. Best of five games.

I made my avatar selection – Eleval Banshee and waited while B'alezal went through a variety of options. The controller looked tiny in his massive claws, but he handled it with surprising dexterity. He settled on Raldar, the character known for shooting lightning out of his guitar and flying. *Great.*

My hands were clammy, and I wiped them on my jeans, trying to focus. I hoped that either the Knights Recumbent would get here soon, or that B'alezal wasn't as good a player as he thought he was. I heard Dan whimper on the couch, and I tried to give him a reassuring look.

"You realize you are going to die a slow, painful death little fey, don't you?" B'alezal said in a gravelly voice that seemed to come out of all the speakers at once.

"Save the trash talk until you actually win, you soul eating scumbag." I gritted my teeth and hit the play button.

"Round 1. Fight," came out of all the speakers, making my hair stand on end, and I started by throwing a chord blast. Caught off guard, B'alezal grunted in surprise. I pushed his fighter back and tried to keep him off guard and on the defensive as much as possible.

It was an ugly first game, and I hadn't played in quite a while. I was rusty. My three lives were gone in short order, as the final 'You Lose' death scene played out before me. Dan turned a shade paler, and B'alezal cackled, a strong sulfur smell overwhelming the room. "Do you want to give up now, little girl?" His voice boomed out of the sound system.

"Just getting warmed up. Last I checked, we still have four games to go." I wiped my sweaty palms on my jeans again and settled in, doing my best to ignore the large stinking demon leaving scorch marks on the couch beside me.

I hit the play button again, and the two figures appeared on the screen. I opened with a chord blast. Little pixilated musical notes streamed from my avatar's fingers, then she went into a combo that, if I completed the sequence correctly, would give me an extra power boost to my next chord attack.

B'alezal grunted and tried to counter, but I was faster than he was this time. The sequence, along with the power chord was enough to down his first life. I won that game, and the next one. The fourth game came around and the score was Katie 2, B'alezal 1. I guess I got sloppy, or overconfident. He took me out in the fourth game faster than a knife through butter.

Dan was still whimpering on the corner of the sofa, and the temperature had risen in the basement enough to make me sweat. This last game would determine Dan's fate. And my own. All told, I thought he was holding up remarkably well. He hadn't run screaming.

This was it. My hands were shaking, and I took a deep breath to steady my nerves as best I could. I hit play. The demon beside me roared, and our two avatars battled on screen. B'alezal was good. Almost as good as me. It was a very close game, but in the end, I won. As his fighter lay on screen going through the death video sequence, I felt sweat dripping from my forehead, my hair plastered to my face.

B'alezal roared and turned, screaming through the speakers. "Cheater! You cheated. There is no way some filthy woman beat me." Flames were starting to, quite literally, shoot from his nostrils, and the smell of burning plastic and singed hair filled the air. The Knights Recumbent chose that moment to make an appearance, and mass chaos ensued.

When the Knights show up, they don't tend to knock politely on the door, they appear out of thin air, fully armed, and usually riding some sort of steed. This was no exception. When B'alezal, angry at having lost, started to turn on me, five knights on horses appeared in the basement. Now, fey horses are thankfully much better trained than their counterparts, but appearing inside a basement with a demon is enough to try anyone's nerves, and they snorted and shied as far back from B'alezal as they could get. Everything was in chaos around us. I grabbed Dan by the arm, and we flattened ourselves against the back wall, inching along until we reached the stairwell.

I watched as B'alezal turned to meet the Knights, all of them comically hunched over in the low-ceilinged room. One of the knights threw an energy bolt at B'alezal, and I turned and shoved Dan up the stairs as fast as he could go. "Up. Now. Outside, as fast as we can," I shouted over the roaring from below. He stumbled on the top stair, and I grabbed him under the arms, trying to help him up.

"Move!" I shouted again. We raced for the front door, and I yanked it open, flinging Dan through it, and myself after him. We ran, our feet pounding on the pavement on the otherwise silent street. At the end of the street, we slowed.

"What… what was that thing?" Dan panted.

"That was a demon. A rather nasty one. It had attached itself to you and was using you to hunt. Also, I hope you have insurance." I bent double, trying to catch my breath.

"Insurance?" he said, confused.

His house exploded, sending a jet of fire twenty feet into the air. "Ah." He jumped and cringed. "Would you mind telling me what in hell is going on here?"

"Well," I said, straightening up. "Demons are real. You were basically playing host to one. I played a videogame to reclaim your soul, and then the Fey equivalent of the police showed up and blew up your house. Probably."

"Ah. So, what you're saying is, I've gone crazy, and I'm actually in a loony bin somewhere imagining all this?" Dan looked around hopefully.

"I'm afraid not. But the good news is, you have two options at this point. You can either keep your memories of tonight and know that the world is a lot bigger place than you first thought it was, and I can introduce you to some local fey that are pretty cool, or I can wipe your memory and the fire department will find you wandering around outside your burning house with no notion of what happened. You can go back to living your regular life if you want to. And either way I'll put a charm on you so that you don't look quite so tasty to demons." I paced back and forth in front of him. "Unfortunately, you don't have long to decide, as I can hear the fire trucks coming."

I paused in front of him. "Which will it be, the red pill or the blue pill?" Looking at Dan a momentary bout of pity struck me. This was one hell of an introduction to the fey world.

He chuckled at the reference, the panic receding slightly behind his eyes. "Well, when you put it that way, I'll take the red pill. Show me what there is to see in this wide new world."

I nodded. "Hang on to your hat then." I whistled a series of three notes and a cab pulled up out of nowhere. I turned to Dan. "One of the perks. Driver, take us to the Dog and Duck."

"Aye miss. Right away."

"So, do you do magic?" Dan looked me over curiously.

"A bit here and there. I try not to rely on it too much. My friends will tell you more though." I stretched and leaned back against the cracked leather seat of the cab.

We arrived at the Dog and Duck in short order, and I paid the cabbie. "Come on. You've got people to meet."

Dan followed me to the back of the pub, and I waved to a group sitting in one of the corner booths. "Guys, this is Dan. He needs to get astoundingly drunk, he's had a rough night, and then we need to show him the ropes. He just got a rude awakening to the fey world."

My friends cheered, and Jocylin flagged the waitress. "An IPA for our new friend please." Jocylin turned to Dan. "Welcome to the ranks of the initiated. We'll keep an eye on you."

The End

"Oh, you're already done? That was quicker than I expected. I was just making space for a new book that will soon be added to the library. The shelves needed to be dusted and cleaned before I add it to the collection. I wouldn't want our newest addition to feel neglected or unwanted. It's rare that I'm able to add new stories these days. This will be the first in years.

I should probably spend some time with the older collection as well – it wouldn't do for any of my precious darlings to feel unwanted. The ink fades if it's not refreshed every now and again. I've collected every single one of them myself, don't you see.

Let me grab another story for you. I'm feeling positively light on my feet with all the energy you've brought into my home. The place hasn't felt this alive in years. You'll like this next one – it's a bit longer, but that will give me time to finish dusting and arranging things while you read. Don't mind the thumping on the roof, some of the shingles are just a bit loose.

I'll try to be quite so as not to disturb you. I feel like you're really getting into the stories more deeply now.

I see that Iktómi finished your shawl. It should keep you nice and toasty. Feel free to scream if you need to – it won't disturb me at all. I would understand. And the next story is a bit scary. An adventure: some might consider it a horror story, others a love story with a twist, I do admire Bert and his persistence in this one – but you'll see. Here's "Year Three". Sometimes the best tales are the ones that send a shiver down your spine.

I'll stir the fire for you, it seems to have burned down a bit. You're cold, you're drained, and I wouldn't want you to catch a chill.

YEAR THREE
(of the zombie apocalypse)

The Redhead's legs went on forever as she stretched at the end of the bed wearing a slinky black negligée. She turned and noticed him on the bed, and with a smile, crawled up towards him. He felt her hands caress the inside of his thigh, her cold eyes staring at him as she sensuously opened her mouth, licking the edges of her red lips. There was something about those eyes... then she began to bleat at him.

Bert groaned as reality intruded with the blaring of his alarm clock. Mrs. Fritz, the cat, was head-butting his knee. He reached down and scratched her behind the ears while he waited for his eyes to focus.

"Man, that dream..., she is so hot. No way she'd ever go out with me though," he mumbled as he sat up in bed and turned on his Pinkey Pop playlist.

Just like U came on and he hit the skip button – all the songs on that album were awful. Pinkey's number one dance hit blared from Bert's surround sound, and he could feel himself waking up. He batted at the mosquito netting covering his bed. Before setting his feet on the floor he checked to see if any vermin had arrived during the night. It would be pretty damn stupid to get bitten by a zombie mouse in his own house. They usually couldn't get past the trays of water his bedframe sat in, but he hadn't survived this long without being careful. It only took one bite after all.

He didn't see any of the tiny telltale wet footprints that would signify mice or rats, so he set his feet gingerly on the floor outside of the water trays. This was southern California so at least it wasn't cold. He stretched and shook his hair out of his eyes. It was getting long again, might be time to shave it off. It wouldn't do to have it getting caught in the equipment. Or worse yet, getting caught by one of them.

He ran through his schedule as he suited up for the day. The first layer of protection, silk long-johns to keep from chafing. First delivery is to that apartment compound. Second unit there, so they know the drill. No hassle with the payments, and I like those two guards, they don't talk much. Heavy-duty pants and tear resistant shirt followed, then the steel toed boots. The daily ritual calmed him and put his mind in order. Black leg armor followed by Kevlar torso protection and then reinforced arm guards for his forearms. Second delivery, down at the docks. Must be careful getting out there; the highway goes right through the petroleum wasteland. Lots of bandit gangs. Need to keep an eye out while I look for the drop point. Signal to find the customer at the docks – The Italian Flag. New customer so they will probably want to be chatty. Dammit, that always throws off my schedule. Last of all a full helmet and neck protection followed by gloves dense enough to withstand a direct bite. Last delivery, a posh house in Beverly Hills. New customer, but last delivery of the day so it should be fine even if they're chatty. Some bandit activity in that area, but nothing too heavy.

He finished dressing as he finished going over the schedule. The eLo™ units he delivered allowed people to store solar energy so they could use it at night, or keep their refrigerators powered, or more importantly their security systems. *eLo™ was great before the outbreak, but our units are a basic necessity now. Our competition can't come anywhere close to what we can do – hah! They wish they could touch us,* he thought with pride.

He was fine on time. The first delivery was only a few miles away, and his truck was loaded and ready to go. Homeowners were given a five-minute delivery window. If they weren't there on time to open their compound gates, he would wait five minutes. He never skipped out at 4 minutes 45 seconds either, that was cheating, and he knew how important these units were to folks. For most, it was literally life or death.

"Five minutes," he mused aloud. It was the length of time before the local Shamblers would come to investigate. If the homeowner wasn't there on time, they would have to reschedule for two months from now.

People rarely missed their appointments these days. Not like at the beginning.

His warning alarm sounded, letting him know he would need to leave in three minutes. He double-checked his gear one last time and looked at the security screens showing his fenced in yard. Bert prepared for the sprint to his armored delivery truck as Pinkey switched to another upbeat dance tune.

He checked all his external video feeds as he unlocked the door. Being a delivery driver had some perks, including a substantial paycheck. With it he purchased the most advanced security system available. It was a good job, but he was looking forward to reaching gold status so he could take a vacation. If today went well, he might be gold by the end of the week. It was a tough goal – 500 successful deliveries.

Shotgun in one hand tire iron in the other he made the sprint. It got his adrenalin running, even though he did it every day. Most people, he knew, wouldn't bother running, but his neighbor down the street forgot to set the lock on his gate two weeks ago and a Runner got into his compound and got him.

You can never be too careful.

Safely locked inside the truck he could see a couple of Shamblers outside the fence. Those didn't bother him too much. *It was the Runners you really had to worry about*, he thought.

The Shamblers didn't appear to have noticed him. Bert shook his head watching them for a moment. He couldn't imagine how awful it would be to be stuck in that state forever, craving the living while slowly (literally) falling to pieces as a mindless shell. Of the three categories of zombies, Shamblers, Runners and Meat, it was the last that freaked him out the most. Meat were zombies so far decomposed that they couldn't even move, they just lay there moaning. *What an awful way to go.* He shook his head, clearing the image from his mind.

Bert ran though the weapon's checklist for his truck. Two shotguns, extra shells, his dad's old Winchester rifle, a couple of tire irons, and most importantly – the safe with the final injection. He keyed in the combination and stared at the syringe full of green liquid with fascination and revulsion. Most people didn't request the injection in their inventory, but he wanted to make sure. If he turned, if at all possible, he'd end himself rather than end up as one of them, as meat. He shivered at the idea.

He put the truck in gear and pulled up his route for the day while fitting ear buds in through his helmet. He loved blaring Pinkey Pop – he never got tired of her stuff. "Still right on time," he muttered, keeping an eye on the clock.

He sounded the loudspeaker before opening the gate, getting the attention of the zombies outside. Sometimes a few Runners hid in the group of Shamblers, and he couldn't risk them getting in. He knew they would bolt for him as soon as they heard the music. Nobody ran today. The zombies continued their slow stumbling about, so Bert hit the remote and opened the gate, driving around the Shamblers. They were easy to avoid, and current laws forbade killing them unless they were actively trying to attack you anyway. No one was quite sure if they had any consciousness left; most people assumed not, but the scientists that were left insisted it was possible. Besides that, cleaning the truck after hitting one was awful.

The GPS directed him down what used to be a main thoroughfare. Thank God the GPS satellites are still up and working, he thought. I bet one of the Redheads had a hand in getting our technology into space. The road was deserted except for a few brave souls; nothing like Los Angeles before the outbreak. The four-mile drive to his first stop took a mere 10 minutes.

As he pulled up at the familiar compound, he surveyed the scene. This at one time had been a high-end gated apartment complex. Now it looked more like a fortified compound. A team of two people, a man with a shotgun and a woman with a homemade flamethrower waited outside the gate. They nodded, and the man said, "Hey Bert, good to see you again."

Bert nodded, waived, and backed the truck up to the gate as he tried to remember the name of the man. He put it in park with the engine running. Sliding out from behind the wheel and into the back of the delivery truck, he shifted open the well-oiled door and used the pallet jack to slide the unit out onto the lift-gate. The lift-gate started its slow descent and Bert saw the two guards tense at the sound. This was the most dangerous part of any delivery. The noise from the truck would attract attention. The humming thrum from the engine increased, and despite well-oiled hydraulics, the sound of metal on metal sang out. Bert cringed internally but kept his face stoic.

The woman said in a low voice, "Two at the east end of the street have turned this way."

"I've got three on my side," the man with the shotgun said, as he chambered a shell. "Runners. They're coming fast."

"Shit." Bert said in his helmet. The unit was a big one and weighed five hundred pounds. He had to wait until the lift-gate touched the ground; there would be no pushing it off early. He looked at both guards. They were steady enough, and well prepared, but he loosened the tire iron on his belt just in case, and reached back and loosened the shotgun from the holster at the back of the truck.

After what felt like an eternity the lift-gate touched the ground. Bert heaved against the pallet jack, running the unit through the gate as a shotgun blast went off beside his head. He ducked reflexively but didn't stop pushing until the unit was well into the compound. A man on the inside gestured to where this little colony of survivors wanted it placed. Bert maneuvered it to the designated spot, dropped the hydraulics on the jack, and held out his hand. The man slapped a keycard into Bert's palm. In one motion Bert pulled out the card reader to activate the unit, swiped the card and took off at a run back towards his truck, towing the clumsy equipment behind him.

He could see the woman with the flame-thrower engaging the two undead, and watched as she doused them in flames. It was an eerie sight – they caught fire and went up like torches, but didn't scream, or make any noise at all. Bert had never liked the flame thrower mentality. Yes, it looked cool, but for sheer practicality, it wouldn't stop Runners, and at best it might give you an extra few seconds. It also ran a high probability of catching the surroundings on fire as burning Shamblers wandered around until they collapsed. He could see three more coming up quickly.

Diving for the lift gate button, he pressed it as he dragged the pallet-jack back onto the truck. The lift started to rise, and Bert grabbed his shotgun to help fend off the gathering horde, firing at a grouping just coming within range. When the gate was back in place, he yelled, "Clear!" as he slid the door closed from the inside. He saw the two guards sprint for the gate, and watched it roll back into place as he breathed a sigh of relief. He reloaded the shotgun and returned it to the holster in the back of the truck, then checked the one that could be easily accessed from the driver's seat.

Sliding back into his seat he surveyed the scene outside. There was a horde of about ten of the undead shambling around, trying to breach the truck walls. Undoubtedly there was at least one under the truck trying to gnaw on the fluid lines – that problem had been solved last year by under truck armor plating, so he wasn't too worried. They were a dreadful sight – pale green, vacant expressions, in some cases missing limbs, or with eyes falling out of sockets as the body slowly decomposed. And universally, the hands –

fingernails turned to claws, and the skin stretched tight over the bones, pulling them into misshapen ghouls. Although he couldn't smell it in the truck, he knew outside the miasma of rotting flesh permeated the air.

He heard a loud thunk and turned to look. A runner met his eyes through the glass, staring. For a brief moment Bert wondered if the tree-huggers were right. Was there someone still in there? Then the with a crash and the sound of fingernails on chalkboard the zombie was clawing furiously at the window on the passenger side of the truck, trying to find a way in; its claws scraping futilely against the bullet-proof glass. *That would be a nope.* Bert thought with a shudder.

He fired up the engine and with a loud 'vroom' that made the entire truck vibrate and pulled out trying not to hit any of the Shamblers gathered around. After he cleared the horde, he fishtailed the truck to dislodge the runner still clinging to the mirror. It lost its grip and hit the pavement. Bert slammed on the brakes and threw the truck into reverse, running over the creature and crushing its head. *One less threat to deal with. And good riddance. And if some tree-hugging idiot wants to put me in jail for getting rid of that abomination I'd like to see them try.*

He checked the time; an hour to get to his next appointment. The next stop was on the other side of the city though, and there was no telling what he would find between here and there. He slid the truck into drive and headed out, Bert shook his head, pondering the overall situation.

Some of the laws the tree-huggers managed to get passed were very strange. The only one that made sense to him was the 'no shooting zombies indoors' law. That one came about when some idiot with a shotgun shot at a zombie in an office and the grapeshot passed through the undead into several of his co-workers. Not only had the zombie not died, the co-workers had, and came back as more zombies. *And*, he thought practically, *legality aside, I don't like to run the Shamblers over - it's hell to get them out of the grille on the truck. Runners though, I'll take the extra hassle to rid the world of those.*

Man, the whole system of government is messed up. The shadow government that takes care of the infrastructure, that's good I suppose, but all the gangs, it's just crazy. Of course, business wise it has some up-sides. I mean if our competition hadn't started paying protection money and then priced themselves out of the market we wouldn't be doing nearly so well. Of course, I hear they can't figure out how we get our stuff made so cost-effectively either.

The drive out to Long Beach took him past long stretches of what used to be city. Ironically, the year after the outbreak, Mother Nature relented and the drought that plagued southern California for two decades had ended. Gentle rains twice a week replenished the reservoirs, but also encouraged the native flora and fauna to grow. Large swaths of the city had been taken over by palm groves and fruit groves, and fast growing vines of all types. Entire city blocks disappeared into non-native forest. Lucky for him, the highways were still clear.

The port cities handled the outbreak differently. Many of those living out here owned watercraft, and when it became apparent society was collapsing, they banded together and created floating towns out of their various barges and boats. Raiding teams would make for the shore once a week or so and hunt or steal food. The fishermen thrived – within two years they were sea based tribal societies. But they still had uses for electricity. *Guess that's why they needed a unit.*

He was going to have to off load the unit, and then work with a ship crane operator to get it on board a boat at the dock. He shook his head. *This is going to be a shit show. Good thing the buyer is flexible. I hope he can follow the plan.*

Bert hit the button on his IPod and turned the music up earsplittingly loud for the rest of the trip. Stressing about the delivery in advance wouldn't do anyone any good.

As he drove past miles of abandoned city, his mind wandered back to the first days of the outbreak. He had been a new employee for a now defunct delivery company and was picking up an eLo™ unit at their headquarters in North Hollywood. A news bulletin came over his radio about a biological accident at a lab in Burbank just down the street. Someone turned on the television to pick up the news, and the reports had been horrifying. Were still, to this day, horrifying. Bert shook his head at the memory. It had been awful.

All the employees at the lab turned in a matter of hours, as had all the rats and mice they experimented on, and plague born by rodents and humans, descended on the West Coast.

Bert wondered if they'd ever found the eLo-solution CEO. He was traveling when the outbreak happened, and as far as anyone knew was still stuck overseas. As soon as the outbreak became known, all fights were grounded. The travel embargo didn't stop the plague of course – rats always find a way. Europe was hit six months later and was having a much harder time dealing with it.

At eLo-solution, in the absence of the CEO The Redheads had taken charge and declared lockdown on the building. That was the first time he had seen her. The quiet one. Bert smiled. *Man, I so wanted to ask her out. Then all this happened. There's no way she'd even look at me these days. She's way too busy.*

He had been inside when the lockdown occurred, and they gave him the option to stay or go. Very few referred to them by name anymore, he knew their names, her name at least, Sarah. But the two women worked so well in tandem, everyone called them The Redheads.

The arguments were fierce, but the two women prevailed. Anyone who left the building wouldn't be let back in. A few people tried it and failed.

They organized everyone, and between their leadership and the ingenuity of the remaining employees, they fought back the horde. The talents that existed in that entire group were amazing. Who knew the finance guy also knew how to build rocket launchers? That one was a real surprise. The Redhead, the quiet one, knew how to lock down the entire building in two minutes. Turns out she frequently worked at night all alone and the area made her nervous, so she knew all the codes and where all the keys were. The two submariners – well, military, what would you expect...

Then came the harder part – fighting back the people who wanted in. eLo-solution headquarters was one of the few buildings with power left in the neighborhood. The Redheads stood firm – no one was allowed to enter. There was one scary moment when everyone thought they'd lost one of The Redheads – no one could find her. Then they discovered she'd locked herself out on the roof by accident. Everyone voted and said she could come back in since there was no way anything else could have gotten out there with her.

Bert shook his head. Man, those were hard days. But I'll give them this, everyone that stayed, lived.

After things settled down, and some semblance of order had been re-established, that was when they started delivering energy independence to people again. They did have to change their motto though as 'Going Green' took on a negative connotation. Only zombies went green - that was the first sign of the infection.

Getting off the highway, Bert focused again. Driving on city streets was always more difficult.

Though it didn't happen often, gangs of the living would sometimes try to hijack his truck, the area and between the highway, the San Pedro piers and the Port of Los Angeles was dangerous. Driving carefully to avoid potholes, abandoned cars, and the occasional Shambler, he navigated his way down to the port. On one side he passed what used to be huge oil refineries, now blackened twisted structures stark against the blue sky.

He shook his head at the sight. Shortly after the outbreak, and for many months following, rioting had been a daily occurrence, and one fateful day a group of homegrown terrorists had bombed the refineries, leaving the city effectively without any fuel supply beyond wind and sun.

Bert could see the skeletons of the giant cranes from a distance and looked for the marker. The signal, the Italian flag hanging from one of the trusses was difficult to spot. Better than the time the signal had been a shoe placed on top of an old-school VW beetle though.

He stopped the truck and scanned the cranes with a set of high-powered binoculars he kept on the dash. There! At the very end of one of the cranes he spotted the green, white, and red tricolor flag fluttering in the sea breeze. He followed the crane arm down with the binoculars to see if anyone was sitting in the cab but was blocked by a building.

He threw the truck in drive and made his way closer. There was an unusual amount of undead activity – several small hordes were feeding. He hoped the end had been quick for whoever the victims were as he turned his eyes away. There was literally nothing that could be done. There was no cure for the virus, and once they had you, you were dead.

Driving around the corner of another building, he found the crane with the flag. Using his binoculars, he found the cab of the crane and swore. It was covered with Runners. He could see someone inside, beating against the glass. He toggled his CB radio to public address and keyed the microphone. "Do you have a radio in the crane?" boomed out of the truck's loudspeaker.

He watched the man inside the crane look around wildly, and several of the Runners head's whipped around. "Do you have a radio inside the crane?' He said again as calmly as he could manage. The man nodded frantically.

"Turn it to channel two," Bert said in reply to the frantic nodding. He switched his radio from PA to channel two. "Truck to crane booth, come in." Static. "Truck to crane booth, come in!" More static. On the third time the crane operator found the channel. "Truck to crane booth, come in?"

"Help! I'm trapped!" A panicked voice came back.

"I can see that, where are your guards?" Bert replied, trying to remain calm as he surveyed the scene. *This is bad,* he thought.

"Dead. Hauled off by another horde. They came out of no-where. Help me, please," the voice sobbed.

"Dammit," Bert swore. The manual clearly stated he was to drive away in situations like this, but he couldn't just leave the man trapped up there. Humans had to stick together. More of the horde had noticed him when he fired up the loudspeaker. He drove up as close as he could and revved the engines, getting the horde's attention. Runners loved a chase.

Sticking his head out the window and waving an arm he shouted, "Fresh meat!" and hit the gas, tires squealing as he peeled out. As he hoped, (and feared) most of the horde followed him. Once he had them well away from the cranes, he pressed a button on his control panel and released a gasoline slick behind him. This came from the fuel reserves rather than the main tank, so he should still be ok to get back to the office. With the concrete doused, he stopped the truck and waited. As the horde got closer, he lit a match and flicked it out the window. The fuel erupted and a fiery wall travelled to the pursuing zombies in seconds. They went up like dry kindling and smelled disturbingly like barbecue. Bert put the truck in gear and carefully circled around the writhing funeral pyre as he drove back to the crane. The horde tried to follow him, but the longer they burned, the less they could move. Luckily there wasn't much out here to catch on fire.

As he pulled up, he could see there were still four trying to get into the crane operator's booth. "Truck to crane, are you still in there?" Bert said over the two-way radio.

"Yes! For the love of everything, help!"

Bert sighed and grabbed his shotgun from beside his seat. This was one of the big cranes used for loading ocean liners. The operator was up there a good way, and a shotgun wasn't useful at this range. He got out of the truck, holstered the gun across his back, and climbed the ladder to the crane's operation deck. He could see the operator huddling inside the reinforced glass and steel case. Somehow the zombies managed to spiderweb the glass on one side, and two of them were beating against it, crazed hunger in their eyes.

Angling so he could shoot the Runners without hitting the glass was tricky. He climbed out onto the edge of the deck, bracing himself against the railing. Lining up the first of the undead in his sights he pulled the trigger. It flew back and fell from the rig. The other three swarmed him, faster than he'd ever seen undead move. He got off one more shot with his shotgun before they were on top of him. His armor made it difficult to maneuver, but he grabbed his tire iron and swung it wildly, connecting with the nearest zombie. Its head made an awful squelching noise as it exploded like a ripe melon, and brain matter spattered across him. The creature stumbled back, taking the tire iron with it. The fourth one tripped over his companion, falling over the edge. Bert retrieved his tire iron and rolled the zombie off the ledge.

He went to the crane operator's booth, trying to appear calm though inside he was shaking and desperately wanted to be back in his truck. "Delivery for American Dreamer. Are you here to get it on the boat?"

The man inside the booth looked at him with incredulity. "What! That's what you have to say? You just drove off a horde of those things, and you want to make your delivery?"

"Well. Yeah," he said hands trembling as he re-loaded his shotgun. "Or I'm going to be late for the next one. So, are you going to take delivery or not?" Bert looked at the watch on his wrist trying to exude a calmness he didn't feel. "You have a name? I've only got a few minutes left at this location. What'll it be?"

"Dave. Um." Dave was trembling inside the booth. "That was intense, man."

"Pull yourself together, Dave. Do you want to take delivery or not?" Bert fell back into routine as his mind tried to process the attack. He tapped on the glass to keep the man's attention. "Focus please." Bert knew it would come across as insensitive, but he was still out here and exposed and though he didn't like to admit it, even to himself, terrified. If Dave wasn't going to take delivery, Bert wanted to be back in the safety of his own truck.

"Um… "Dave looked shaken, and his pupils were dilated to huge dark pools.

"Ok Dave, why don't you go back to your boat, and re-schedule for the next available date. Do you want me to walk you down?" Bert felt something grab his ankle. He whirled around and shot point blank the zombie that had crawled up the outside of the rig. Its head exploded in a shower of blood and gore. Bert heard Dave whimper.

"Come on man. Let's get you out of here before they come back." Bert turned around just as another zombie crashed against the spiderwebbed glass of the operator's booth. It caved inwards, slamming Dave against the control panel with a sickening thud as the zombie scrabbled, trying to get through it. Bert grabbed the ankle of the creature and pulled, heaving it as hard as he could over the edge. The foot came off in his hand as the rest of the body sailed into emptiness. Bert shuddered and dropped the foot, kicking it over the edge as he tried not to heave up his breakfast. Dave was staring in surprise, head at an unnatural angle, eyes glazed over in death.

"Dammit." Bert shook his head and ran to the edge, adrenaline racing through him. Zombies were gathering below, and a few were scaling the rig. It was a large group of Runners.

"Shit and fuzzballs next time I'm following the manual."

It was too far to jump. He pointed his shotgun down the ladder and pulled the trigger, clearing out three of the creatures. Several more were coming fast. He fired again, trying to clear a path. When he'd discharged all his shells, he reloaded from his belt and started down. Pausing halfway he had to fire again to clear a path.

When he was close enough, he jumped to the ground and sprinted for the cab. Dead hands grabbed at him, and grotesque fingernails slid off his helmet. For a moment he panicked, flailing wildly, arms swinging wide as they connected with the runner that jumped on him. Then he was inside the cab of his truck. He slammed his foot on the gas pedal and heard his tires squeal as he raced out of the area.

"Shit, shit, shit, shit shit...." He drove, heart pounding, until he reached the highway and made it to an overpass. When he was in the clear he stopped, flung open his door and stumbled out of the truck. He spewed what little was in his stomach all over the roadway and heaved for several minutes, mind blank. When he came to, he took stock. He was covered in gore, heart still racing, with a failed delivery he would have to report. He felt like this attack had been worse than most. The zombies hadn't been this active in nearly a year.

Eyes wide he checked all the mirrors to make sure there were no Shamblers or Runners in sight; then used his decontamination kit to wash as much of the gore off as he could. The smell of rotting flesh made him gag again and he threw up bile. Splashing his face, to rid himself of as much of the smell as he could, he felt runnels of water making their way under his armor. He hoped it wasn't also carrying the splatter down into hard to reach places. The suit was great protection, but it trapped heat, and out here it was pure misery by mid-day. Normally it was fine, but normally he didn't have to scale rigs and fight off hordes. Checking his watch, he swore as his hands shook. He was going to be late for his third appointment.

He closed the water can and scrambled back into the truck, radioing the office. "Bert to home base. Come in base."

"What's the code?" A static filled female voice came over the comm.

"Code 8245." He put the truck in drive and started down the deserted road.

"What's the problem Bert?" the voice replied.

"One of two – notify my third delivery of updated time window. Delivery time is now eleven fifty five A.M."

"Confirmed – updating delivery time with customers. Are you en-route?"

He could hear the bustle of activity in the background. "Yes, en-route." He swerved to avoid debris in the roadway as he pressed his foot on the accelerator. "Two of two – reporting an attack and failed delivery at the docks." He shuddered remembering the horde crawling up the sides of the crane.

There was a pause in the static. "A failed delivery and an attack? Any injuries?"

"The point of contact for the delivery did not survive. I saw evidence of other recent attacks but cannot confirm who the victims were. The horde was quite large and very active. Recommend declaring area off-limits for the immediate future." He could feel his hands still trembling against the steering wheel. Looking down the road he thought he saw a barricade of some sort crossing the highway.

"Shit," he swore softly. Barricades meant nothing good. Probably pirates. There were a couple of different types he might be dealing with – just a local territorial group trying to keep people out, no big deal just avoid them; gangs out to conquer territory and cause mayhem; or the worst, funded corporate pirates, paid to ensure that only certain company's goods made it through, or to stop goods from competitors. The crackling of the radio interrupted his thoughts as he slowed the vehicle. *Take the off ramp, or power through the barricade?*

Likely the ramp was the trap, but the barricade looked pretty solid. Making a quick decision he turned the truck around, glad everything in the back was well secured, and headed back the way he came.

"Bert copy?" came over the radio.

"Please repeat," he said as he checked his mirrors to see if he was being followed.

"I've notified third delivery of updated schedule. They have confirmed. Please file a report on delivery two when you return this afternoon. Stay safe out there." He heard the radio click.

"Copy that home base. Any reports of Pirates on the 101?" The spot between his shoulder blades itched. He was missing something.

"Not recently. Last report was a month ago." The radio popped and hissed at him.

Hmm. Then he heard it. The 'whump, whump' of helicopter blades. "Home base, I'd like to report pirates on the 101. They have a helicopter. Heading for the surface streets now. Wish me luck!"

"Good luck, Bert, we'll see you at debrief this afternoon."

He muttered under his breath, "You bet your ass you will." He pressed the accelerator to the floor and sped down the nearest off ramp, letting his GPS re-route to the last delivery. Pirates didn't normally have helicopters – this smacked heavily of a funded group. Funding meant corporations. *Shit. The truck's not built to handle the heavy stuff,* Bert thought, frantically trying to remember if there were any good side streets in the area.

The helicopter was hot on his tale, and he heard the 'pop pop pop' of gunfire, and the pings as the bullets bounced off the armored vehicle. The best way to lose them would be to head into the Los Angeles jungle. Between the concrete and the trees, it would be hard for the helicopter to see him.

He headed inland. The truck, while perfectly capable of fending off bullets, and zombies, wasn't really equipped to stop armor piercing 30MM shells. He reached 80 mph and felt every small imperfection in the road, bouncing and rattling as he raced along, the chopper still right above him. Downtown loomed faster than he would have thought possible, and the trees thickened, hiding the sky. He raced down the narrow streets, still in the direction of his delivery.

Gradually he stopped hearing the ping of bullets and the whump of the helicopter blades.

On the far side of downtown, he breathed a sigh of relief. The helicopter had vanished. Let's hope is stays gone, he fumed. Dammed corporate pirates. It's not like the regular groups can afford military grade equipment – heck, I can't even really blame the regular gangs, everybody's gotta eat, but these corporate guys are vicious.

He checked his watch. The pursuit slowed him down, but he still had just enough time to make the new delivery window.

***

Bert pulled up outside a carved marble and iron gateway with more scrollwork and flourishes than Buckingham palace. He double-checked the address. Most of the rich and famous either died or left during the first year of the outbreak so Bert was surprised to find himself in the Beverly Hills area at all. This was certainly the largest mansion he had ever seen. He looked around but there was no one waiting at the gate. "Shit."

He pushed the call button and polite voice said, "Who is it?"

"This is Bert from eLo-solution. You have a delivery scheduled for today."

"What's an eLo™?" The disembodied voice asked.

"It's a battery-based energy storage system for your house. So, you can have power when the power goes out," he responded patiently. "Miss, you have three minutes left in your delivery window. Or you will have to reschedule."

"Let me double-check the delivery schedule for today." There was a brief pause and the sound of papers rustling.

"No, I'm sorry, we don't have any deliveries from eLo-solution scheduled."

Bert checked the address on his screen. "Is this 10236 Charring Cross Road?"

The woman's voice answered, "Yes. But I assure you we didn't order whatever it is your delivering."

Bert swore softly under his breath and put the truck in reverse. His five-minute warning light was flashing, and something was definitely fishy. The backup sensors beeped as he started moving, and he hit the brakes, looking at the rear cameras. He couldn't see anyone or anything that would be causing sensor to go off, so he started the truck moving again. Suddenly, he heard a loud bang and felt the backend of the truck shudder. "What now," he muttered.

He angled his side mirror to try and see the back of the truck. It looked like one of the tires had blown a hole. Without pausing to investigate further he threw the truck in reverse and peeled out as best he could, the run-flat tires digging into the pavement. Four cars pulled out after him, all of them made for speed, all of them silent electric cars. Bert was glad he had paid the extra money for the good tires, but even as durable as they were, the damage would slow him down. Two of the cars cut him off and forced him down a narrow alley. He slammed on the brakes when he realized the alley ended in a brick wall. The truck was solid, but he didn't think he should take on a building. Bert swore put the truck in park and made his way to the back. He rolled open the door and grabbed his dad's Winchester rifle. Bert smiled, he and his dad had many arguments about shotgun vs. rifle and Bert still held that for zombies, shotgun was the way to go. But these very obviously weren't the undead. Standing behind one of the eLo^{TM} units he took aim at the lead car and fired.

The narrowness of the alley was a mixed blessing. While he had little room to navigate his truck, his pursuers had little room to dodge his bullets. The windshield of the first car shattered but the driver kept coming. Bert calmly unloaded a round into the car and chambered another round. The car spun out of control sliding to a stop directly in front of him. He could see the driver's, brains splattered across the dashboard. The passenger was still moving and slid out of the car and out of view. The other car screeched to a halt and two men with assault rifles opened fire. Bert ducked as gunfire pinged in the inside of his truck. These were definitely not your standard Pirates.

He heard the clatter of feet on the roof of the truck, and voices as one of the men conferred with another. "Don't hurt the unit; we need it for research purposes."

Bert fired his rifle up towards the speaker and was rewarded with a yelp of pain.

The smoke grenades will be next, he thought. Sure enough, a rattle on the floor alerted him as a grenade came rolling into the back beside his foot. He kicked it out the door and ducked back as gunfire started up again. The gunfire stopped and through the deafening silence he heard one of the men shouting. "Come out with your hands up and we won't kill you."

"How do I know you're not lying," Bert replied.

"You don't. But would you rather take a chance on maybe surviving, or dying for sure?" One of the men shouted.

"Who sent you?" Bert replied.

"Let's just say your product has caught the attention of a powerful competitor. I'm sure you understand." The voice seemed to be moving closer.

Bert tried to track where the voice was coming from by sound, but his helmet muffled his hearing. With the smoke obscuring his vision it was hard to tell. *If I were sneaking up on me, which way would I come? Along the alley wall or behind the car?* A slight sound from the wall to his left made the decision for him. He stood and fired through the smoke. He heard a grunt and the thud of a body hitting the ground. *Three down. How many were there?*

The sudden sound of gunfire and a burning sensation ripping into his arm told him there were more out there. Bert ducked back behind the units as gunfire rang through the interior of the truck. He felt a burning sensation on his arm and looked down. A slow stain trickled out from under his armor. Then the true pain hit, and he gasped. He struggled to sit up and reached for his safe as he passed out, wondering who would make his deliveries in the morning.

***

An hour later Bert stood, shook his head in confusion and moved to the driver's seat.

Oh god what happened? Was I shot? I think I was shot. Bert checked, and he did seem to have a bullet hole in his arm. It had stopped bleeding and didn't hurt nearly as much as he expected. He felt around his ribs and found another wound. It was clotted and sealed. He sighed with relief. *I guess they missed hitting anything important...I must have passed out from shock.* He tied up his arm with a tourniquet just in case though. His ribs still hurt, but he could check that damage later.

He rose and looked around his truck. Holes peppered everything, and one of the eLo units was gone. They had obviously left him for dead. He returned to the driver's seat and started up the truck. Thankfully it started on the first try. He'd been half afraid the engine might have been shot out, but it seemed fine.

He backed the truck out of the alleyway cursing. *I've got a pretty good idea who those guys were, and dammit they got an eLo™. Hopefully they put enough holes in it that they won't be able to get any useful intel.*

Bert gripped the steering wheel angry enough to see red. *I can't believe they left me for dead. You don't leave someone helpless for the zombies to find. That's not just corporate warfare, that's inhuman. They must have seen the blood and thought I was…The thought* lingered in his head. *Wait.* Bert slammed on the brakes. *They put a bunch of holes in those units. They put at least one hole in me… What if… No, I'm thinking much too clearly. I mean…* He put the truck in park and went to the safe and keyed in the combination. He looked at the final injection, and then looked at his bandaged arm. *But I feel normal. I mean, normal and recently shot, but still normal. I'm fine… right?* His hand hesitated and wavered over the injection. "Caught between life and life's choices" the lyrics to an old Pinkey Pop song came to mind and he hummed the music along with the sound of her voice in his head, then smiled. *Wait, if I can remember song lyrics, then I must be fine.* He gave a nervous laugh and went back to the driver's seat.

The deliveries had not gone well, he had to drive back on a flat tire, and he would have massive amounts of paperwork to finish while they loaded up the truck for tomorrow. And there was no way he was going to make gold status this week and get that vacation. Bert shook his head. He hoped tomorrow's deliveries would be easier. He sighed and mouthed the eLo-solution employee motto. Dependability, Reliability, and Dedication. Energy for all. *See, I must be fine. Already thinking about paperwork.*

He radioed the home office to say, "Truck C42 to base, on my way in for the day."

A voice replied, "What was that? Please repeat."

Bert tried again, "On my way in for the day."

The line went quiet. Then a different voice came over. "Bert, report to homebase."

Bert clicked acknowledgment on his radio. For some reason his radio didn't seem to be working. *I guess it caught a bullet too.*

Bert studied his hands on the steering wheel. They still looked normal to him. How would he know though he wondered.

He put some Pinkey Pop back on his headphones, but a nervous fear crept up his spine. What if he had turned, and he just didn't know it? How would he know? What if all those poor Shamblers out there thought they were still normal and didn't understand why their neighbors suddenly started attacking them? Bert shook his head. That was ridiculous. Now he was just making stuff up. Obviously, he hadn't turned, he was driving a truck – who had ever heard of a zombie driving a truck? Bert chuckled and turned the iPod up. Of course, he hadn't turned – blood loss was just making him loopy.

As he headed back to base he glanced around the inside of his truck and shook his head. It was a mess. Bullet holes everywhere, his gear in tatters, holes in the windshield. *Man, resupply is going to have a field day with me. I never realized how much heat this truck kept in during the day. Couple of little holes in the truck and it's freezing.*

He pondered the cold for a minute and then widened his eyes in a panic "Oh God," his mind spiraled. "What if it's not actually cold and I'm just... dead." The trip back was miserable as Bert over analyzed every little action, every sensation. "Am I dead? Do I give myself the injection? Am I just loopy from blood loss? How do I know?"

Bert was in such a muddle that he got lost twice on the way back. He sighed with relief when he finally managed to pull into the parking lot. Backing the truck in the loading dock he stepped out, already preparing his report in his head. He swiped his badge across the security lock and walked in.

Perky, the office manager screamed. Bert looked around in a panic, that girl had a set of lungs on her. He decided he must not have cleaned off the gore from the zombie attack earlier in the day. "Perky it's okay, it's not my blood." Her eyes bulged and she screamed again, backing away.

"Okay, Okay, I'll go clean up. Calm down." Bert headed for the bathroom and the decontamination showers.

***

Bert gave himself a once over in the sink. He stopped when he saw himself in the mirror. 'Well, no wonder she screamed,' he thought. I look like death warmed over. I probably would have screamed too. He poked at himself nervously. Maybe I *am* death warmed over... He felt his finger poking his face and chuckled nervously. No. Definitely not. "Geeze, get a grip man.

I'll have to see I can take a few days off. I wonder where the HR director is."

He opened the door, and all his coworkers were standing around outside the bathroom.

"Guys, seriously? There are two other bathrooms in the building." He shook his head and shrugged, making his way to the service desk to file his report. Everyone took a step back when he moved, and he rolled his eyes. "Do I really stink that badly? What, have you all suddenly run out of work to do?"

No one answered, and more than a few of them looked at him nervously.

He filled out his report and handed it to the delivery specialist on duty. The man took it gingerly and backed away. Bert smiled at the shipping clerk. "Have you got my delivery schedule for tomorrow?"

The shipping clerk paled and nodded to someone standing behind Bert. He felt the rope drop over his shoulders and around his arms before it tightened, pinning his arms to his sides. Flexing his arms, he tried to loosen the loop as one of his co-workers comically ran around him in circles winding the rope tighter.

"What? Are we doing a zombie drill now? Again? We just had one last week. Come on guys, I've had a really bad day." *And shouldn't HR have told me I was the zombie this time?*

His co-workers roughly prodded him with brooms, one person pulling on the rope, leading him towards a conference room. Bert knew where they were going – one of the meeting rooms was isolated, they'd stick him in there until management called an end to this. Bert closed his eyes, whimpering, still holding out hope, but with a sinking feeling of confirmation. He was surrounded by pale faces and looks of terror. This wasn't a drill – his co-workers were going to kill him.

They shoved him in one of the small conference rooms, and he heard the door latch behind him. The room had a small table with chairs for meeting with clients, but not much else. There was a mirror on the far wall to make the room look bigger, and a painting of the Rocky Mountains to put people in a good mood. Bert caught sight of himself in the mirror and did a double take. He moved closer to get a better look.

His skin was a pale pasty greenish color. His clothes were covered in dried blood and bits of gore. His mind processed that for a moment. He was going green around the edges. 'Oh my God,' his mind screamed. I've *have* turned into one of them.' His legs gave way and he fell landing in one of the conference room chairs. He shuddered at the sight of himself. He knew what was coming next. Someone, eventually, would be coming through that door injection in hand to put him down like a dog. *But I'm still me! I'm still in here! I don't want to die!*

Bert started shaking with fear. How could he let his coworkers know he was still Bert? That it was still him, not some mindless beast. That thread ran through the head as he tried to figure out when he'd been bitten. Certainly, the zombie swarm had been brutal, but he didn't remember any bites that got through his armor. The events surrounding his last delivery were hazy, but there was no doubt that he'd been shot at least once. He checked his clothing and was surprised to find his armor had several holes in it in critical places, and that most of the blood seemed to be his.

Bert guessed that he must not have cleaned off all of the gore from the zombie swarm, and when he was shot, he became infected. That would explain why it took him so long to turn.

"Dammit," he said, wanting to cry. Though that's not what came out, even to his ears. I was very nearly to gold status with the company. I'm never going to get to take my vacation now. And I only needed three more successful deliveries to get there. Somehow this upset him more than he expected. He worked hard for that vacation. He earned it, and now it was being taken away.

Then it hit him again. "Oh God, I'm actually dead. This is it; this is what lies beyond." He gulped, uncertain of what to make of the revelation. His thoughts spun off in a million directions at once as his mind tried to encompass the enormity of what had happened. To ponder the slow disintegration of mind and body, only – he wouldn't have that either. A co-worker would be coming in soon to finish him off. The next coherent thought surprised him. Who was going to take care of Mrs. Fritz now? Mrs. Fritz was an independent little cat, but still, she did need her food and occasional petting.

***

Several employees stood outside the conference room door looking nervous as a red haired woman wearing a black suit and heels came down from the executive offices. She had a grim expression and carried a large syringe in one hand.

"I'll go in and check on Bert and if the final solution is needed, I will administer it. Davin, please remain here, the rest of you wash up, sanitize just in case – you know the drill."

***

Bert heard the click of the door latch, and he spun around in the conference chair. His eyes were immediately drawn to the large syringe in The Redhead's hand. His redhead's hand. Then he registered that they had sent one of The Redheads to give him the final injection. He vaguely thought he should be flattered. The Redheads were always incredibly busy keeping the company running.

She advanced on him slowly, speaking in a calm voice. "Now Bert, this won't hurt a bit, I promise."

Bert froze in place, and babbled, "Oh god please, I just wanted to go out with you." He immediately wanted to slap his hands over his mouth, and slowly started backing his chair away, rolling until it hit the wall. The Redhead smiled and shook her head. "We'll see. I think I'm free Tuesday next week. Bert, I promise. This won't hurt a bit, and you'll be better afterwards. You're going to have to trust me. I know you're confused right now, but it will all be better." She spoke in a quiet voice, as one might to a child who was frightened, but continued to advance on him, syringe in hand.

He threw up his arms in a panic, trying to fend her off. She grabbed his arm and jabbed the needle into his neck, depressing the plunger. "Noooo! No stop!" he yelled, "It's still me I swear!"

"Well, I know that," she said practically, withdrawing the syringe. "That's why I'm here."

"Wait. What? You can understand me?" Bert looked around wildly and then blushed. "You. Understood. Me?"

"Of course. You've had your injection." She smiled and continued. "Now, what I injected you with was a lab created spinal fluid serum. The serum lasts about two months, and then you'll need to get another injection, or you'll go back to being green."

"Wait, what?" Bert rubbed his neck, trying to rub out the feeling of the needle going in as he looked around.

"Hush now. There are a few things I need to tell you before I can let you leave. First," she paused, staring directly into his eyes. "You're dead. But so am I."

Bert stared at her, trying to put the pieces together in his mind. He was pretty sure he was dead, but she couldn't be dead. It didn't make sense. She nodded, seeming to understand the thoughts going through his head.

"You remember that day I got locked outside? Yeah. That's when it happened. I was bitten. But before I could change, another one of the unliving got to me and gave me the injection. The injection I just gave you."

"So, it's a cure?" Bert asked. His voice already losing the raspiness of death.

"No. Think of it more as an evolution. We need the spinal fluid to regenerate our cells, but we look as normal as... well, as them." She tossed her head in the direction of the office. "There are several of us about, working here, but you have to keep it a secret." She leaned back and smiled. "Being one of the non-living has some great perks. We don't need to sleep, we never get tired, we're stronger than the living, and if someone pisses us off, we can turn them into a zombie." An amused look crossed her face. "Best yet, there's only a few ways we can die. We do have to get regular injections though, or we turn into one of the mindless masses. Welcome to the club."

Bert's eyes widened at that. "But so... was that one of the syringes from off the wall? From the zombie kit?"

The Redhead frowned and shook her head. "No, those actually will kill us. What I gave you was from my special stash. I'll make sure you get some to tide you over. When the tree-huggers managed to pass the vote about how to kill us indoors, they also specified what had to be in the syringes. And quite frankly, if someone is too far-gone, or too far decomposed then we do use those as a mercy killing. Some sacrifices have to be made." The Redhead smiled and held out a hand to help him up. Bert ignored her, still reeling.

"There are some other perks too – people who have a certain talent, when they become one of us, their talent seems to increase. It's pretty spectacular. That artist you like so much – Pinkey Pop? Yeah, do you remember the awful album she released right before the outbreak?"

Bert shuddered, "Yeah, 'Far Out Body.' It was awful."

"You remember the album after that? Released about a year later? The one that stayed at number one for six months. We turned her in the interim. She got much better."

Bert shook his head. "Seriously? You mean you non-living are everywhere? You all …"

"Bert," she interrupted him. "We. Not you all. You're one of us now. Welcome to a whole new world. A world where we control the energy."

Before he could say anything, The Redhead turned and opened the conference room door. "It's all right folks, Bert just lost a lot of blood. Looks like our competition funded a small army to get one of our units. He's going to take a few days off and be back in next week."

Bert watched as his co-workers cheered, feeling numb. The Redheads ran a tight crew, and he was happy he could stay on. He looked around and noticed

Brad, the eLo™ installation trainer, was staring at him intently. He didn't know Brad well, their paths didn't cross often, and he found the man to be overly gregarious for his tastes, but when they locked eyes, Brad gave him a slight lopsided smile and nodded in welcome.

Bert's eyes widened, and he nodded back, grinning. The Redhead smiled and walked with him to the front door. Let's get you a ride so you can get yourself looked at. Take a few days off, and we'll see you next week."

***

Two weeks later Bert backed his truck up to a heavily fortified gate. Two men with shotguns met him and told him where to make the drop. He nodded, looked at his watch and prepped the units for delivery, whistling along to a Pinkey Pop song blaring from his stereo. As he brought the unit to the ground the two guards stared at him nervously. "Let's get this unloaded and taken care of. I need to get out of here on time tonight boys, I've got a date with a redhead."

The End

I've always liked Bert. He was a good soul.

Snuggle up in that cozy chair, there's no reason for you to move around much. The fire is going, you have your tea and scones. Let me add a pillow here for you. The light is just right at this time of day to read the pages clearly.

We're quickly coming up on my favorite part.

But, silly me, this is all about you – what's your favorite part I wonder? Well and here I am nattering at you. Let me just look and see what story to pick out next.

I think… here it is… I think you'll enjoy this one. "The Assistant," it's got mystery, excitement, and the joy of friendship and teamwork. Oh, I'm so glad you're here. Perhaps we'll be friends in the end.

THE ASSISTANT

I scowled in a mixture of concentration and frustration. I was carrying twelve lattes, all customized, with three trays of four drinks each stacked and balanced in front of me. The faces of the men I passed walking through the trade show floor were a combination of impressed, concerned and amazed. One very lovely gentleman held open the heavy convention center door for me and I wished many blessings upon him as I was simultaneously cursing my boss. I had been an assistant at various levels and to various people for more than a decade, but this guy took the prize in the crazy department.

By rights we shouldn't even be at this trade show. A week ago, we hadn't even had a booth, but Emory made that part happen. Then Daniella and I scrambled to get everything coordinated and pulled together. It was only the first day of the show and I was ready to drop. I was sure Daniella felt the same, but Emory seemed to have some sort of magic ability to talk people into things. It was most apparent when he was selling but anyone who worked directly for him felt the effect. My coworkers commented on it often enough.

The trade show floor opened just as I arrived at the booth and was swarmed by a small army of salesman. Everyone helped get the coffee into the right hands and then we were off to the races for the day. I didn't have a specific role in the booth. I was there to keep an eye on everyone and everything and get Emory to his meetings on time. This type of coordinated chaos was my jam and the hours sped by. I made sure everyone got food and water and took care of themselves while always keeping sight of Emory. Daniella helped coordinate all the press interviews, and requests that were coming in. Today seemed to be going well and Emory had not yet made any wild demands, so as the close of the show day approached, I started to relax.

"Anna!" I heard Emory's voice behind me. "Well done today. You and Daniella are really pulled this off!" He sounded genuinely pleased, so I arranged my face into a smile before I turned around. Despite how it might seem on occasion, I liked Emory quite a bit, but he had the ability to get on my every nerve.

"Thanks, it was definitely a team effort I'm really glad we hired Daniella when we did," I replied.

"Yeah, she's a good addition," Emory agreed. "So, I know we didn't talk about this in advance, but I'd really like to reward the team for doing such a good job at the show today. Do you think you could get a dinner reservation for tonight somewhere not too far from the hotel?"

I looked at my boss dubiously, disbelief creeping into my tone. "A reservation for tonight for twenty people during a major trade show, with no notice?"

"Yes! I know it's a hassle but I'm sure you can pull it off. Let me know where you decide on!" He smiled encouragingly and I sighed. I should have anticipated this. He wasn't going to accept no as an answer in any case. After a dozen or more phone calls, and searching around for options on my phone, I called in some favors and got the group into a private room at a bougie pizza parlor that had an excellent beer selection. Everyone seemed happy and there were no complaints about the lack of hard liquor. I swear sales teams run on nothing but coffee and alcohol.

By the time everyone was done I was falling asleep in my seat. The next two days of trade show were non-stop talking to customers and pitching product with barely any time to eat or rest.

When I showed up at the downtown office on Monday I was still exhausted from the weekend and even though I'd slept a full ten hours the night before, I didn't feel rested. I pounded back a vitamin drink just in case I was coming down with something and hurried in to the office.

Everything looked and sounded normal. The office was bustling, and people were where they should be. Still, I had this lingering, nagging feeling that something was wrong. Waiving the feeling off, I chalked it up to coming down with a post-convention cold and plowed through.

By Wednesday afternoon I was sure I had the flu.

"Emory, I'm going to be out sick tomorrow. I don't know what this bug is, but I don't want to give it to everyone." I said, coughing into my elbow, and feeling a flush of heat followed by chills.

He looked up from the computer at his desk, and smiled, but I could see the annoyance in his eyes. "I hope you feel better soon," he replied. "It's important to take care of your health." He had learned the right words to say, but his tone was dismissive, and he immediately went back to the screen in front of him.

I nodded and closed the door. There really wasn't anything else to say, so I went home for the evening. Forty-eight hours of sleep helped and on Saturday I was looking forward to driving out to the country to visit with my friend Laney.

Laney and I went to junior high together, and although our paths had diverged wildly, we still got together a few times a year to hang out in the outdoors and commune with nature. Laney liked to style herself as a witch.

I didn't believe a word of it but everything around Laney was calm, and we always had a good time. I tossed some jeans and a few sweaters in an overnight bag and headed out of the city. It was an hour's drive to Laney's family cabin in the mountains, so I grabbed a coffee from Good Vibes, my favorite coffee shop before hitting the highway.

Latte and orange cranberry scone in hand I felt ready to face the drive. I was exhausted but not as much as I'd been two days ago. It was early; the sun peeking over the horizon. The mountains, and fresh clean air beckoned and I reveled in the silence of the drive and the absence of work demands. The ascent was stunning and by the time I reached Laney's doorstep I was starting to feel freer.

Laney was not an early riser, so I wasn't surprised that I was the first one to the cabin. I'd been here often enough and knew where everything was. The cabin was far enough off the beaten path that her family never bothered to lock the doors. When I was younger this freaked me out, but Laney explained. The cabin was remote. There were almost never any people out this way, and if there was someone out here and they needed help or shelter they were welcome to come in. The family didn't want anyone dying of exposure due to locked doors. There had never been any issues, and occasionally someone would leave a note thanking them for the shelter.

I took a moment to look over the cabin. The exterior was made from rocks collected in the surrounding area and carried here over a period of years. Guessing, I'd say the place was probably a hundred years old. The stones held up well, and Laney and I and a few friends had re-roofed the place last year. It was hard work but ultimately not complicated. It was only a three-room cabin after all. I was pleased to see the roof seemed to be holding up just fine.

I let myself in and brought in armfuls of wood. The weather called for light snow, but it was spring, so the possibility of heavy snow was always the danger. The cabin was primitive – no running water, heated only by a wood stove, and with minimal electricity. After stocking the wood, I emptied the water storage jugs and pumped new water into them. The storage containers had been sitting here for a while, based on the coating of dust, and there was no reason to drink stale water. By the time I had a fire going and water in the kettle I heard the rumble of Laney's car coming up the road.

I dropped tea bags into two mugs, one for each of us, and sat down in the battered old lounge chair by the fire. A few minutes later Laney came breezing in her arms full of grocery bags. "Anna! Up early as always," Laney said cheerfully. "Let me grab a few things from the car and I'll make breakfast,"

I smiled. Laney's sunny disposition was always refreshing. "Need any help?"

"Are you kidding?! I can see that you've been doing all the heavy work. Sit down and enjoy your tea I'll only be a moment."

After being sick, I reluctantly acknowledged that I might have pushed myself too hard. As I sat down with gratitude, an overwhelming wave of exhaustion unexpectedly washed over me.

What seemed like only moments later, I was smelling frying bacon and eggs. I opened her eyes to see Laney standing over the wood stove stirring a frying pan full of that heavenly smell.

Laney glanced over and smiled. "You doing okay? I came in from the car and you were sound asleep. You didn't even move when I took your teacup out of your hand."

"Wow. How long was I asleep?" I asked, stretching.

"Nearly an hour, and I was not being quiet."

I shook my head. "I've been fighting something for the past few days. I thought I was past it, but I guess not."

"Well. Let's get some food into you, and then later today we'll do a healing ritual. I'm pretty sure I have the right herbs with me. We'll get you feeling normal again."

I smiled at Laney. "You're the best. Now tell me, what's up with you. Are you still dating that guy from last fall?"

Practically inhaling my eggs and bacon, I listened as Laney caught me up on her love life. She made another cup of tea and sternly told me to stay put while she gathered the items she needed. I didn't follow Laney's religion, but Laney had performed healing rituals before, and the brothy soup that was part of it was tasty and nutritious, and resting by the fire was all I had the energy for at the moment anyhow. I must have fallen asleep again because the next thing I knew, Laney was leaning over, shaking me gently by the shoulder.

"Anna, wake up. Drink some of this," Laney said, thrusting a steaming mug into my hands. I took the cup reflexively and held it to my lips, sipping carefully. Laney was staring down at me with concern.

"Girl, I don't know what you've gotten yourself involved in, but your aura is all messed up. It looks like something has been trying to eat your spirit, one small bite at a time. It's no wonder you're so tired," Laney said shaking her head. "Until we get more information on what's going on I'll make you a basic charm against evil. Unless you know something already?" she asked hopefully. I shook my head, bemused and still somewhat befuddled from sleep. "Something is eating my spirit?" I replied, questioning.

Laney rolled her eyes in frustration. "We have talked about this before. I know you're not a believer but I'm not crazy. I can see your aura, and it's had giant pieces ripped away."

I shook my head, willing my eyes open, trying to wake up and focus. I trusted Laney. She'd always been there for me. "Okay. Break it down for me like I'm a total ignoramus, which in this case I am. I trust you, and if you say something's wrong, then there's something wrong." I yawned, still hampered by the exhaustion. I wasn't thinking very clearly, and repeated, "Did you say something is eating my spirit? What can I do about it?" I asked leaning forward to carefully set the mug on the hearth.

"Well, I assume you don't know what's doing it?" Laney said tentatively.

I looked at her amused. "That would be correct. I can't remember the last time I let someone eat me." Laney's eyes widened her nostrils flaring as she looked at me. I looked back eyes crinkling at the corners and we both broke into helpless snickers.

"Ohh God. Phrasing. This is serious, Anna," Laney said as she tried to stop snickering. "We should investigate getting that problem fixed for you too but that's a different potion. Drink your soup," she said, plucking the mug from the hearth and putting it back into my hands.

"Okay so we're working against an unknown at this point. I'll put some basic protections on you. How do you feel about me visiting you in the city for a few days? See if we can get rid of this thing?" Laney asked.

"Sure. My new place is tiny but I'm always happy to have you around. You haven't come to the city for a visit in a long time," I replied.

Laney nodded. "Good. It's settled then. Here, put this on for now." She slid a hemp bracelet that had beads woven through it off her wrist and onto mine. "Whatever you do, don't take it off. Just like a seat belt, it can't protect you if you're not wearing it," she said with sternness. "Now, it's midafternoon, and not too cold out. Whatever is attacking you isn't here. How do you feel about a short walk in the woods before it gets too dark? Get your blood flowing again."

Tired as I was, I smiled. "That's what we're here for after all. Let's see what's changed since last time." I levered myself out of the chair waiting for a faint wave of dizziness to pass before following Laney to the door.

By the end of the day Sunday, I was feeling much better. Even so, Laney insisted on coming back with me. My place was more like a bungalow than an apartment, or almost a tiny home. It was built in the 1930s and survived as a rental unit. At 500 square feet - one bedroom, a living room, a tiny dining room and tiny kitchen, it was cramped, but it had character. What it didn't have was central air and central heat. For heating I relied on a little potbellied wood burning stove. It was rustic for the city, and probably against code, but it was a lot cheaper to heat with wood than electricity anyway. During the summer months it didn't get too hot, and when it did, I could always go out to visit Laney in the mountains. Instead of a table I had a futon in the small dining area, so I pulled it out and set it up for Laney to sleep on. I had to be at work early on Monday so said goodnight and headed to bed.

Laney called after me, "Don't forget to always keep that Talisman on you. I don't want anything taking any more bites out of you!"

"I promise!" I replied crossing my heart as if I was still twelve.

It was nice getting into the office early. Everything was quiet and I had at least an hour before everyone else came in. Within ten minutes I had the coffee percolating. It wasn't part of my job description, but I drank it as much as everyone else and if I made it at least it would taste the way I wanted it to. Wandering around the office I turned on all the TVs showing the updated sales numbers and got Emory's desk set up for the day.

Emory's desk had a strange, red gritty substance scattered over the surface. Almost like some sort of sand. Grabbing a wet paper towel, I cleaned it off and wiped down all the surfaces carefully. Throwing the wet sopping mass into the trashcan, I felt a shriek building up. The paper towel looked like it had been drenched in blood, and when landed in the bottom of the can it made an unpleasant splat sprinkling drops of the reddish liquid everywhere.

In the bathroom, I doused my hands in soap and was relieved to see that whatever it was seemed to be washing out easily. I double checked to make sure I hadn't splattered any on my face or clothing. I didn't want to look like a murder victim in the office. My hands were shaking at the unexpectedly gruesome mental image. By the time I had the mess cleaned up, other people were coming in for the day. It was a busy day, and I never got the chance to ask Emory about the red dust. At home that evening Laney took one look at me and 'tisked' like a grandmother.

"What happened today?" she asked.

I recounted the incident from this morning and Laney shook her head. "I'm not familiar with that, but it sounds... not great."

"I washed it all off as far as I can tell," I replied. "If I'd been thinking, I would have saved some of it for you to see."

"Are you feeling okay?" Laney asked, concern tinging her voice. "Just as well that you didn't bring any of whatever it was into your house – there's no telling what it might bring in with it."

"Pretty normal. Just tired after a long day. Do you want a glass of wine?" I asked, squelching the annoyance I felt building. Laney was trying to help, there was no reason I should be annoyed at her.

"That would be great!" she replied enthusiastically. "Since you had to work all day, I figured I'd cook dinner. I hope you like Mac and cheese - the fancy kind!"

My sudden annoyance vanished as quickly as it had appeared at the words Mac n' Cheese. "Are you sure you don't want to move in with me full time?"

Laney laughed. "Let's figure out what's trying to eat you first - this seems like a dangerous city to be living in right now!"

Over dinner - made marginally healthier by the addition of green peas to the Mac'n Cheese, Laney told me about the wards she'd added to all the doors - these were designed to keep unwanted spiritual beings out.

"I also put crystals on all the windowsills," she said, around a mouth full of shells & cheese. "They keep out a different kind of supernatural critter."

The addition of the crystals gave my bungalow a very different aesthetic. During the day I imagined there would be little rainbows everywhere, bouncing off the walls. I smiled at the thought; rainbows were always cheery.

"I need to head to bed early tonight. Clients coming in tomorrow, so another early day for me." I said, as we finished up dinner and cleaned everything up.

I arrived at the office just after 6:00 AM. Emory expected everything to be perfect, and I wanted a few minutes to myself before setting up. Walking in, I was surprised to find the alarm wasn't armed. "Hello?" I called flipping on lights. There was no answer. Sighing, I figured the cleaning company had forgotten again. I'd have to speak to them about that.

Walking up the stairs to the conference room next to Emory's office, carrying an armful of corporate swag: pens, notebooks, and fancy water bottles, I thought I heard voices in low conversation. The lights were out in the hallway, but I could see a faint glow through the frosted window of the CEO suite.

I dropped the swag in the conference room without bothering to turn on the lights and walked quietly to Emory's office to investigate. At the door, I could clearly hear two voices; Emory's and another that was much deeper. I crinkled my nose as an odd smell hit me; it was almost like a gas leak - rotten eggs mixed with something else. I'd need to bring in some air freshener or fans.

It was strange for Emory to be in the office this early in the morning, and even more unusual for him to be in with a client. He was *not* a morning person.

I heard the voice say. "Your last offering was quite delectable. But I have not received payment in several days. Your time is almost up." The words sent shivers down my spine, and the hair on the back of my neck stood on end.

Emory replied. "I know and I'm not sure why my deposit yesterday didn't go through. She must have worn gloves or something when she cleaned up the mess in my office. I may need an extension. I must use the gift you gave me today when my clients arrived to secure this deal." Overhearing that, I felt sick. I was the only one who he could have been referring to – even the cleaning staff didn't have a key to his office. What was he up to? I wondered.

"I have no interest in your petty business deal. You made an agreement. I will give you until the end of the week to pay and now double the amount. Either you provide payment, or you will be the payment." The glow from Emory's office winked out, and the weird smell vanished at the same time. Startled, I realized I was lurking and hurried back to the conference room, hands trembling.

What did it mean that Emory had tried to use me as 'payment'? It certainly sounded like Emory had gotten in over his head with someone. I took several deep breaths. I needed to compose myself. It would not do for Emory to realize I'd overheard that conversation.

Our customers arrived promptly at 9:00 AM. I was surprised this client had even accepted the meeting. Just last week, their CEO sent a very angry e-mail denouncing the quality of our product and threatening to get lawyers involved, and today we were sitting down to negotiate a potential partnership. Emory had asked me to take notes on the key points from today.

I studied the players at the table. Their CEO was a petite woman with dark hair who sat ramrod straight in the conference room chair. She was flanked by her entourage, their head of sales on one side, her assistant on the other.

"Welcome, everyone. Thank you for coming all this way to meet with us." Emory said, smiling broadly. His smile was met with stony stares and polite nods.

When Emory started giving the corporate pitch, I watched as our guests' demeanor changed. They went from cold and disinterested to leaning forward in rapt attention. They seemed fascinated by Emory's presentation. He was always a very engaging speaker, so I wasn't surprised. To my eyes though, today he seemed off his game. His words fell flat on my ears. I was distracted though. Laney's charm bracelet, made from some sort of hemp string, had started itching and a red welt was forming anywhere in the string came in contact with my skin.

During a break I gave Laney a call. "OH MY GOD Laney. What is in the hemp on this bracelet? I'm having some sort of allergic reaction or something," I said, holding the phone to my ear and trying to scratch at my wrist at the same time.

"Wait! What? Take a picture and text it to me right away," she replied, her voice tinged with excitement.

"If I hang up on you, I'll call back." I held the phone with my off hand, trying to take a picture awkwardly without dropping the phone or canceling the call. "OK, here it comes." I waited impatiently for the image to go through. I never had good reception because of the mountain range, a problem everyone around here understood.

"OMG Anna, you need to get out of there immediately. Someone you're in close contact with today is our culprit. So far, the bracelet is doing its job. Do Not take it off, no matter what."

"I can't leave! Emory would fire me for walking out of this meeting!"

Laney sighed impatiently. "Anna? — Something is trying to EAT you and it's in the office. Do you really want that job?"

"Laney, rent is due next week. I cannot just walk out. I have to stick it out at least until the end of the day." I said, as my stomach roiled with anxiety.

Laney's voice crackled on the line. "Fine. I'll have some soup ready when you get back, and then you're going to tell me everything that happened today and do not take off that charm."

"I gotta go. They're all coming back to the meeting," I replied, hanging up hurriedly and hiding my inflamed wrist behind my back. Emory looked frustrated and glanced at me as he walked in. I wasn't sure what happened during the brief break. Our guests seemed perfectly pleasant and were smiling as they sat back down. Pouring everyone another round of coffee, I sat down to take notes again. To my surprise, Daniella walked in.

Emory greeted her warmly and turned to me. "Anna? Get out. Your presence is no longer needed. Daniella will take over from here." His voice was cold and hard, unlike his usual pleasant demeanor.

I gave Emory a dubious look but did not contradict him. "Sure. No problem. I'll see you in the morning." My stomach knotted even more, as I collected my things and made a hasty retreat.

He waved me out impatiently. Daniella looked as shocked by his behavior as I felt but sat down and opened her laptop to take notes. I closed the conference room door behind me, shaking my head. Daniella would do just fine, but this was very out of character. I shrugged, grabbed my things and headed for the door. Laney would be pleased to see me home early at any rate, and Emory hadn't fired me, so I'd still be able to pay rent at the end of the week. Hopefully we'd be able to resolve this crazy situation. Although.

I paused, thinking. Could Daniella be in danger?

She was our new Office Manager, and I didn't know her very well yet. We worked together and had a pleasant working relationship, and I certainly didn't want anything to happen to her. I also didn't know if Laney's charms would even work on anyone else. As I stood pondering, seized with indecision, the meeting broke up and everyone came filing out. They had wrapped up what had promised to be a very long meeting in only fifteen minutes.

Emory looked jubilant. "Anna! You're still here. Good! I was just telling Daniella — we need to plan a party for Friday afternoon. We'll have the official contract signing and handshake then. We'll do it here at the office, but you two will oversee pulling it all together. This will be the biggest deal we've ever signed." He looked down at my inflamed wrist. "OH, and don't wear such unprofessional jewelry into the office again. We're a business, not a hippie commune."

Daniella was the last one out of the conference room, and she seemed exhausted and subdued. Her face was pale, and her lips had a strange blueish color to them. It was an extreme change from her demeanor just fifteen minutes earlier. I linked arms with her as if we were the best gal pals in the world and whispered, "Are you feeling OK?"

She shook her head. "I don't know what's come over me. I'm exhausted and dizzy. As if I've run a marathon."

"I've got a friend making dinner at my place. Why don't you join us? She always makes enough for ten people."

Daniella looked over at me, eyes dull and dubious. "How did you stand being in there all day? That was so intense!" She replied, leaning on me.

"Yeah, OK, you're definitely coming over for dinner so we can talk," I replied.

I could tell Daniella was about to fall over, so I grabbed her purse and led her to my car. "Come on, I don't live too far. We'll get some food into you." I texted Laney that we'd have one additional for dinner and pulled out of the parking lot, still scratching at my wrist. In just the short drive back to my place, Daniella fell asleep. I pulled into the tiny driveway and shook her shoulder.

"Wake up! Here we are!" She opened her eyes and looked around dazedly.

"I don't know what's come over me," She yawned and rubbed her eyes. "Ohh, what a cute place!" She said, once her eyes were focusing again.

Laney opened the door, peering out into the gathering twilight. "Ah, and there's my friend. Let's go inside," I said, grabbing our things.

Daniella nodded and wobbled a bit as she opened the car door. Laney came out and hustled us in, closing the front door firmly once we were inside. She shot me a look behind Daniella's back, clearly asking what the heck was going on. I said, "I told Daniella all about your excellent soup recipe. She's having a day today like I was last week. I was hoping you wouldn't mind if she tried some of it." I hadn't been able to tell Laney much via text other than we were having an additional guest.

Laney's eyes widened and understanding. "Ah! Yes, of course I made enough for all of us. It's lovely to meet you."

We got Daniella situated on my couch. My tiny bungalow was feeling very crowded with three people in it, but it smelled amazing. Laney dished out three mugs of soup and kept up what seemed like inconsequential chatter about her jewelry business while we ate.

Since I was pretty sure she didn't have a jewelry business, I just smiled and nodded and played along. Then I saw where she was going with it. We needed to get a charm on Daniella.

"Ohhh, you know that piece you showed me yesterday would look perfect on Daniella," I exclaimed. "Do you still have it?"

"Let me run grab it from my things," Laney hopped up and went and rummaged through her bag. "Here we go! This will look just great on you!" Laney said enthusiastically, dropping a pendant on a silver chain over Daniella's head.

"Ohh, but I can't possibly," she said, starting to take the necklace off.

"Nonsense," I replied. "It looks great on you. I'll buy it for you as a thank you for all your help last week at the show. Now, how are you feeling? Can I get you more soup?" Daniella looked flustered at all my questions.

"Better. Thank you. The soup was delicious. I'd love another serving if there's enough." She twisted the pendant in her fingers. "Why are you being so nice?" She asked nervously.

I gathered from her tone that she been on the wrong side of corporate politics more than once in her career. "Honestly? You seem nice and I don't want you to get hurt. Emory can be overwhelming, and I want you to protect yourself from his crazy. It helps to have allies in the office."

She looked dubious, but sad. "He is a bit much, isn't he?"

"He is, and you must set boundaries early and firmly." I shook my head. "It's something I had to learn the hard way. You don't have to let him walk all over you."

"He doesn't seem like the type to respect boundaries," she said nervously, looking around as if she expected him to pop out of the woodwork.

"It sometimes takes being determined about it," I replied, but eventually he does learn. "Also, I appreciate having another woman in the office. There aren't that many of us."

Daniella nodded in sardonic agreement at the last statement. "Right?! So much testosterone!"

"So. Let me buy you something pretty My friend gets paid, you get new jewelry, and I get to say thank you. It's a win all around and you'll wear it to the office."

She nodded in agreement, and I dropped the chain back over her head, the pendant hanging nicely with her work blouse. "Good, that's settled."

"I appreciate you looking out for me, I'm still new to the area and I don't know that many people yet," Daniella offered with attentive smile.

"We should make time to hang out outside of work. I'll show you around," I replied enthusiastically. "But for now, alas, we both have work in the morning, and I don't know about you, but I'm exhausted. I can either drop you back at the office or call you a rideshare home. What's your preference?"

She looked down at her watch, noticing that it was past midnight. "Oh wow, it's later than I thought. I'll call a car to get home. It's only a few blocks from here. I live close enough to the office that I can walk in when I want to." She pulled out her phone and set up the pickup from the rideshare app. "Looks like my driver will be here in five minutes. Thank you so much for dinner and for this lovely necklace." She stood, grabbing her things, and hustled into her coat.

"I'll walk you out," I said, grabbing a light jacket. "And you're welcome. We'll do it again when we're all less exhausted." Once Daniella was safely tucked into her rideshare, I returned to the bungalow.

"Thoughts?" I asked Laney hanging my jacket up.

"You were right to bring her home with you, and good job getting that protection on her. Let's hope she keeps it on. Now let me see yours."

I raised wrist, still red and itching, though not as much as it had been earlier. "Hmm." She held up an old fashioned, gold rimmed monocle and examined me through it. I was hard pressed not to giggle at the sight.

"Hush. I know it looks ridiculous," she said. "It was the best I could do on short notice. It doesn't look like whatever it was took any more bites out of you. It seems to have gone after Daniella instead."

While she was examining me, I relayed the rest of the day's weirdness to her.

"It sounds like he's made a pact with some sort of demon that has to be fed on a regular basis. Can you get me into the office so I can look around?" Laney looked up from my wrist, the question written clearly on her face.

I thought about it and realized that Emory had unintentionally given us the perfect cover. "Can you stay here through Saturday?" I asked. "Emory wants us to throw a party on Friday to celebrate closing this deal and it would be totally normal for me to bring in a temp to help with that. We could even pay you."

"This would give me good access to the office, and we need to rid the world of whatever this is. It's targeting people in your office, and we can't just leave

209

it roaming free to do harm. I'll move some things around on my schedule."

The week passed quickly — Daniella, Laney, and I working on party preparations. Laney replaced my hemp bracelet with one of silver, and I was pleased to see Daniella wearing her necklace, but we had no further incidents during the week. Laney was frustrated because she hadn't found anything in the office, even when I snuck her into Emory's suite of rooms.

"Maybe it only for a limited time? Or like three wishes or something?" I speculated.

Laney shook her head. "It sounded much more like 'Deal with a Devil'," she replied. She opened a document called *Laney's Grimoire* on her computer that had all sorts of arcane drawings and pulled up a page titled *Deal with the Devil*. I raised my eyebrow at her, and she shrugged. "Welcome to the 21st century. No more lugging around heavy books."

She studied the page on the screen. "Since I didn't even get a good look at Emory, it's really hard to say, but from everything you've described, this is it."

"The party is tomorrow, Emory will, of course be there," I said, stretching and trying to relieve the tension in my lower back. I felt the vertebrae pop and some of the muscles relaxed.

"Make sure you wear your protection," Laney said absently, still studying her document.

I nodded, shaking the bracelet on my wrist. "Are you done putting together your charms for the rest of the guests?" This wasn't really something Daniella or I could help Laney with.

"Not yet, but they'll be done by tomorrow," she said absently, chewing on a fingernail as she squinted at the screen.

The party was tiki themed. Laney built her protection charms into the Lei's we'd be handing to everyone as they came in. "Okay, I'll pick up the tiki torches in the morning and the DJ and catering should be good to go. We'll kick off at 5:00 PM."

I was up and out the door by 6:00 AM, yawning and willing my caffeine to kick in faster. Knowing there was plenty to do before the event, I was the first person in the office. In the dim pre-dawn light, I couldn't shake a sense of unease, as if the air itself carried a weight of foreboding, as if someone lurked just beyond my sight. Pretending I didn't notice anything, I started whistling a cheerful tune badly and went about turning on all the lights and brewing coffee.

Soon, the ominous feeling passed, and I was able to start organizing our party favors. Once there were a few more people in the office, I made a supply run to our local hardware store for a dozen tiki torches and fuel. We had a lovely outdoor patio area in the center of the building, more like an interior courtyard, open to the sky. A corporate plant company came by once or twice a week to keep the plants healthy, and it looked enough like a tropical jungle to be a perfect location for the party.

I worked through the day getting chairs, a small stage, the tiki torches, and tables set up. Daniella was wrangling the caterer and DJ, and Laney was taking care of the protection spells. Both arrived at 3:45 for final preparations. I was relieved to see both of them walk through the door.

I ran them through the rough agenda.

"Ok ladies, so I'm going to kick it off with a brief welcome and introduction, and then I'll hand it over to Emory for his final pitch speech. Probably a lot of excitement, but not a lot of substance at this juncture. After the speeches, we'll take the CEO's up to the podium for the official signing. I've got the portfolios here." I handed the two leather cases to Daniella.

"Can you be in charge of those until the time comes?" I asked her. She nodded and tucked them under her arm.

"After the signing, we'll open the buffet, and the DJ will give us some music. If anything weird happens, if you see anything strange or out of place, let me know right away." This was directed to Daniella. We hadn't figured out a way to warn her without sounding like lunatics. The idea of witches and demons and creatures roaming the earth outside of fantasy novels wasn't exactly mainstream.

As the guests arrived, we made sure that everyone received a lei. Emory's was the only one that didn't have protection woven into it. The tiki torches were burning at intervals throughout the courtyard, giving off a welcoming festive light, with a set of them framing the front of the stage. The buffet looked amazing. Piled high with sushi, musubi and a variety of other delicacies, the caterer had outdone themselves.

Getting up on stage, I felt butterflies in the pit of my stomach. I looked out over the audience. There were at least 50 people in the courtyard – a mix of employees from both companies. A nervous smile on my face, I stepped up to the microphone. "Welcome everyone! We are very excited that you are here tonight to help celebrate this momentous occasion. I am pleased to introduce our CEO, Emory Delaney, who would like to say a few words." I smiled and stepped back from the microphone, waving my hands in Emory's general direction.

He bounded on to the stage full of energy, exuding charisma from every pore. Stepping up to the microphone, it gave it a loud squeal of feedback, and everyone jumped and covered their ears. Emory glared at the equipment and stepped back slightly. The squealing stopped. He looked over at me and I shrugged. "Well, the room is small enough, and I can project. No need for a microphone," he said with a hearty chuckle.

Launching into what should have been a great cheerleading speech to get everybody hyped up about the new partnership, his pitch fell on deaf ears and failed to inspire. I'd seen him give this type of speech a thousand times over the years, and tonight, something was very off. People in the crowd were restless and not paying attention.

Emory could tell that he didn't have their attention and as if he turned a dial, I felt the waves of charisma coming off him intensify. The crowd started to get rowdy. I stood near the stage, close enough to witness the fear that crept into Emory's eyes as he fought to regain control of the crowd's attention. He was at a loss, as if he lacked the experience of truly captivating an audience, as if he'd never presented before in his life.

He was pale and sweating when I heard a familiar voice. The voice Emory had been speaking to in his office that early morning a few days ago. "I warned you. You have failed to meet the terms of our agreement. I demand payment. Immediately." The resonant voice was coming from directly behind me. "And since you cannot provide it from amongst your guests, I will take it from you directly."

Emory stumbled back from the edge of the stage, a look of wild panic on his face as a creature straight out of nightmare strode past me onto the stage.

The Demon... It must have been a Demon... Was at least seven feet tall, with skin the color of glowing embers. His eyes were brilliant, blue — the color of searing flame. He wore nothing but a loincloth — which didn't do much to hide his massive muscles and the barbed tail that lashed behind him as he walked. If I'd been one of those girls who was into urban fantasy erotica, I would have found him terrifying, but gorgeous. As he walked on stage, he reached out and grabbed Emory by the face, fingers digging into his cheeks and forehead and his booming voice said, "I must feed." As he did so, Emory's face began to wither, and his skin shriveled.

I had not expected this. Even with all the preparations we had done, I had not, in my heart of hearts, expected a demon to appear in the middle of a corporate party. But there was no denying what stood on the stage.

Frozen, I watched in horror as Emory shrank and decayed in front of me. Movement from the corner of my eye caught my attention and I saw Laney waving frantically. Backing out of range of the stage, not wanting to draw attention to myself, I joined her and Daniella in a clump of ferns. "I hadn't thought he would be quite so big," Laney whispered. "Once he's done with Emory, he's going to go after the guests, and when he finds they're all protected, he'll leave and start attacking random people on the streets," she said in a panic. "We've basically unleashed a demon on the city!" She wailed quietly.

"Think! Can we fight it? We can't let it leave here. No way are we going to let it attack the city! Clearly your protection charms are working. Is it vulnerable to anything?" I asked, glancing back to the stage. Emory's body was starting to crumble.

"Can we... I don't know... Somehow attack it with the protection charms?" I asked.

Laney looked at the lei I was wearing and then glanced over my shoulder and said slowly, "If we wrap the leis around the tiki torches and then surround him. Make sure the charms are on fire and he's directly in the smoke…but we're going to have to stab him with the torches and I'll have to try and banish him at the same time. I think it could work. If not, we'll have to improvise."

"We are out of time," I whispered. "Emory just crumbled to dust." I looked around frantically, gauging our options. "Daniella grab that torch. Laney, get to the other side of the stage. I'll go for the one in front of the stage and try and distract him. You guys come in from the sides." Daniella looked extremely pale, but didn't argue. I heard someone in the crowd scream.

"Now!" I shouted and sprang towards the Tiki torch in front of the stage.

"Hey! Big ugly!" I shouted at it. "I don't believe I've seen your invitation. This is a private party." I waved the tiki torch back and forth menacingly.

The demon turned, looked at me, and laughed. It was a creepy sound that sent frissons of fear down my spine. "Oh. I recognize you. I've tasted you before." His massive hand reached for me, and pivoted, evading him temporarily.

Laney reached her torch and yanked it out of the ground, peeling off her lei and wrapping it around the torch's head. It burst into colorful flames. I dodged out of the way of another swipe from the demon and ripped my own lei off doing my best to get it wrapped around the torch. I succeeded in catching it on fire, but it was not very secure. I thrust my burning torch at the demon - who laughed. "You think fire can hurt me?"

"Would you suggest I just give up and die and not try anything?" I replied as I saw Daniella running up behind it. I needed to keep him distracted. She had a dozen Leis in her arms, and she scattered them in a semicircle behind the demon, lighting them on fire with her torch. I jabbed at him again, forcing him to retreat a step and then another into the semicircle. When the smoke touched him, he screamed.

"Fire, No. Enchanted smoke, yes," I replied. Laney, having seen what Daniella was up to, had collected several more Leis.

Unexpectedly, the demon, in a giant leap, sprang over my head, landing behind me. I whirled to face him, coughing as smoke from the lei at the end of my torch blew back in my face.

"Clever girl. That's why you taste so good," he growled. "But now you've left all these people unprotected. Whatever am I to do? It's so nice of you to set up a buffet just for me."

Horror seeped through me. If he got his hands on any of the guests, they were as good as dead. We couldn't let that happen. "Come at me then! If I taste so good. Here I am!" I shouted, waiving my arms to keep his attention on me. He advanced a step, and then another, as I watched the lei on the end of my tiki torch crumble to ash and float to the ground.

He smiled wickedly, teeth seeming unnaturally sharp. I could swear they grew as I watched. "Ah, not so protected now," he purred, advancing toward me.

I backed toward the stage, and the burning semi-circle on the stage, cursing. It was the smoke we needed, and the ventilation was blowing it the wrong direction. Laney, popped out from behind one of the cocktail tables, arms full of leis, and started throwing them at the Demon's back. The first one sailed wide, but the next one caught on one of his horns, dangling like some absurd drunken party game. He whipped around, and the lei flew off. Laney continued throwing the party favors, forcing the demon to back up, back towards the smoke from the fire on stage. I scrambled out of the way and began collecting the leis that missed their target.

When he had backed up to the edge of the stage, I piled my armful of leis on the ground in front of him and lit them with my now guttering torch. With the enchanted smoke surrounding him, he began shrinking and withering, much as Emory had. Laney began chanting in a language I didn't recognize, throwing the last of her leis into the burning pile. He tried to dodge past, but I forced him back, thrusting one of the burning charms at his face.

"A deal! Let's make a deal! I can make you rich!" he begged. He was now the size of a cat. "Please! You can have anything!"

"You tried to eat us. No deal," I replied as he faded out of existence with a small pop. There was a moment of relative silence, where the only thing I heard was the crackling of the fire and the sickly-sweet smell of burning flowers and then behind me, the crowd erupted into applause. I've been so focused on the demon, Laney, and Daniella, that I jumped in surprise. One of the guests ran up with a fire extinguisher and put out the remains. I looked over at Laney and Daniella and beckoned them to join me at the front of the stage, then, as if we had all been a play or production of some sort, we bowed, and the crowd shouted and applauded. Under her breath, I heard Laney ask, "What now?"

"For the moment, pretend it was all planned until we figure out what to do," I replied. To the crowd, I smiled and waved and said, "Thank you so much! We're going to get cleaned up, please enjoy the buffet!"

Safely locked in the ladies' room, I indulged in a fit of shaking. Daniella was throwing up, as Laney held her thick red hair back. Fear affects everyone differently.

"How did you know that would work!" I demanded, fighting hysterics.

"I didn't. Good thinking Daniella, using all the Leis," Laney said, patting her on the back.

I took a deep breath. "OK, ladies — we've had our moment. We can have another one later, along with several strong drinks. Let's get cleaned up and go deal with the guests."

Daniella looked wide eyed. "There is no way I can go out there and pretend this was all a show," she said flatly.

I took a deep breath. "Laney?"

"I'll come with you, but I'm just a temp as far as they're concerned. You're in charge now, Anna, at least for tonight."

"Crap. Okay." I took another deep breath, washed the smoke off my face and hands, and reapplied my lipstick. "I'll have a proper freak out later," I muttered.

Emerging into the courtyard, I was pleased to see the guests mingling over the buffet. The DJ had some pleasant Hawaiian music playing, and everyone was acting as if it had been a show. Snagging a glass of champagne from the bar for a little bit of liquid courage, I scanned the room. The other CEO's assistant was coming my way. I vaguely remembered that her name was Maki. I plastered a smile on my face and took a large drink.

"Very impressive performance tonight, Anna," she said, smiling. "My CEO wondered if you had a moment to chat, as it seems Emory is ... unavailable." This was our most important guest tonight, so of course I had a moment to chat. I nodded and followed her to a table in the corner.

The petite, dark haired woman sat at the table alone, sipping a mineral water. "I'm very impressed by you, Anna. I know now how Emory convinced us of this deal. Despite how we arrived at this stage, I would like to sign the contract with only a few minor adjustments. But with you, not with Emory."

The woman had a knowing look in her eye. "I heard what the demon offered you, and you did not take it. Honest. Ethical, and determined. I also recognize that this was not a show put on for our entertainment. That was a Magaki demon, very dangerous. Given your actions tonight, I am willing to trust you. Shall we sign?"

Though I was shaking inside, I nodded my head and smiled. "Let's make a deal."

The End

Anna and her friends did good work there.

You seem to be acclimating to the library well. Your binding is coming along nicely. Tightly woven, sturdy – I can see you'll be a colorful one. Yes, yes, it's normal for it to feel a bit stiff at first. You'll get used to it. Iktómi always does such a lovely job.

Everything is going a bit dim? I see the sun is going down outside. Let me light the candles behind you, you've spent all day here reading. Your eyes must be getting tired. You can rest them soon.

You're feeling a bit parched, too? Oh, we can't have that. I'll get you another cup of tea. Something stronger this time – I wouldn't want to dilute the last of the ink. It looks like our newest addition to the collection is almost complete and I want it to have a strong ending, not something that fades over time.

Some people become stronger with adversity. Others turn adversity to their gain, lemons to lemonade if you will – stories teach us that. Some people use adversity to learn more about the world around them and it opens their eyes to previously unforeseen possibilities. I'll be curious to hear which path you think the heroine of our next story, "Yet We Sleep, We Dream," takes.

Do drink your last cup of tea before it gets cold.

YET WE SLEEP, WE DREAM
DREAMSCAPE 1

"Tamara, come here. You must take your pills."
She loomed over me as I scrambled to the far corner
of my bed, huddling in the corner.

"I don't want to!" I shouted back at her tearfully.
"They make me sleep, and bad things happen when I
sleep!" I was terrified of what lurked on the other side
of the door to my subconscious. I hadn't slept in two
days; the terror was so overwhelming.

My adoptive mother never understood. She and
her husband were foster parents who took me in until
the state could place me. When that time came, they
decided they wanted to be my new parents. It's not
like they weren't trying. They sent me to therapists to
help me with the nightmares. As frustrated as they got
with my short temper and constant illnesses due to
lack of sleep, they were trying. I know that now. They
just could not understand why sleep was so terrifying,

and try as I might, I could not convey the absolute and utter horrors that lurked there. The screaming terror that I couldn't wake up from, the suffocating presence that waited for me. These were not things that normal children had to deal with. And so, the doctors prescribed me sleeping pills when I was ten years old.

Fast forward to my teenage years – I became a master of hiding those pills. Dropping them when no-one was looking, holding them inside my cheek until I could spit them into the toilet, leaving them under scraps of food on my plate where they wouldn't be seen. Anything to stay awake as long as I could. My birth mother had died in her sleep, I was only five when it happened. I was the one who found her body, lifeless in bed.

As awful as that had been, it wasn't the reason for my nightmares. Not these nightmares.

At fifteen I began experimenting with drugs. One of my friends at school was taking medication to keep him focused. He hated taking his meds too, so one day he gave me his pills – and I discovered that they'd keep me awake for hours on end. I soon became a willing recipient for his unwanted drugs.

By the time I was seventeen I had found my own suppliers for something better, that kept me awake longer. It had a name - Speed. Unfortunately for me, the human body is not meant to stay awake for days at a time.

One day I misjudged how much I was taking – or I got a bad batch. I'm not sure which. What followed changed my life. I was entirely all too awake as they transported me to the hospital, but I couldn't move. I remember falling, and hitting my head, and the lights of the ambulance, and then the nurses and doctors as they worked over me in the emergency room. Later, my parents joined the doctor at my bedside, and I heard him say,

I heard him say, "Her brain function is erratic, and we need to stabilize it with Propofol." I heard my mother ask, "Is she going to be okay? Is it safe?"

"We don't have a choice," he responded. "She needs to go under, now." I saw him motion to the nurse and she put an IV bag on the stand next to me. That's how I ended up in the hospital in a medically induced coma. That's really where this story begins.

***

The Dreamscape opened before me, a swirl of confusion. Sound took physical shape, neon colors rioted across my vision, pink chasing green chasing blue. I could taste light and feel smells. Sensations I never experienced before. My brain rebelled at being led down the path of madness, the confusion and chaos of it all. Slowly, ever so slowly the scene before me settled into identifiable shapes. The wild colors receded and senses out of order resolved themselves. Then, without warning everything changed again, dropping into blackness. When I could see properly, I was on a city street that looked as if it were straight out of a film noir. The colors all dimmed to black and grey. Lines became sharp and edged. Everything was dingy. Streetlamps created murky pools of light surrounded by deep shadow. And I could feel it. I felt it deep inside of me. That horror, that horror that stalked me in my sleep. That looming, ever present horror. Death.

I screamed at myself, "This isn't real!" and yet, it was too real. It was real enough for my fear. I unconsciously moved into a pool of light, somehow feeling it might be safer than the shadows.

I felt it before I saw it, a shape at the end of the street. Robed, cowled, and with a scythe, silhouetted in the flickering flames of a streetlight, the classic figure of Death.

My breath caught in my chest, as the old, familiar terror of my childhood washed over me. I wanted to escape, I wanted to wake up, and nothing worked. Panic set in, and I found myself racing down the street, into the shadows trying to escape the looming figure.

"Stop!" a deep, booming, voice shouted from behind me. And I quite literally couldn't move. My feet rooted themselves to the ground, my body refused to obey; my every sense screamed out to run, to hide, to get as far away as possible and yet I could not.

Faster than the blink of an eye, Death appeared beside me. It swung its scythe, and I screamed, expecting to feel the kiss of metal on my exposed skin. Instead, I heard a loud clang as the scythe blocked a sword that would have taken my head off my shoulders. I hadn't seen the other presence.

"No!" the deep booming voice shouted, causing the pavement to tremble beneath my feet. "You can't have her." The scythe swung again, as Death engaged the foul creature, stepping in front me, putting itself between me and the darkness. I heard the clang of blade on blade, the repeated hiss of metal through the air, in a battle fought all around me. I could only make out figures, moving amongst the shadows as they battled. It was chaos pure and simple.

And then silence, just as suddenly as it had begun, it was over. There I was again, alone with Death. "Take my hand, child. We must not stay in this place. It is not safe." A hand extended from the robe. I hesitated, surprised. The hand looked like a normal hand, but strong and feminine. I peered through the darkness of the cowl trying to reveal the face beneath. "Child. Come now. We have no time for this," the voice demanded. Death demanded.

Screwing up all my courage I asked, "If I take your hand, will I be dead?"

Thought I could not see a face, Death's voice softened. "No Child. It is not yet your time. But if we stay here, we will both be in danger. I will take you to a safer place."

I gingerly took Death's hand. It was warm and strong, with rough calluses across the palm. "No matter what you see, do not let go, or you will be lost in the Dreamscape." Then suddenly the world melted around me again. Unlike my entry into this place, which had been like an LSD trip, full of psychedelic colors and music, and in contrast to the world of darkness which had formed shadows and harsh lights of a deserted street, this time, everything around us was twisting and warping, colors running like crayons left out in the sun too long. It reminded me of some artist I had seen in one of my schoolbooks and the barrage of melting colors made me sick to my stomach. I clenched my eyes tightly, finding comfort in the darkness.

A few moments later, I heard Death speak again. "We are safe here."

I cracked open one eye cautiously. We were in a clearing in a forest, with a small stream running along one side. Soft sunlight filtered through the trees. It seemed…almost idyllic. But best of all, it wasn't moving and didn't seem to be melting. I took a few deep breaths, and then turned to face Death.

I felt my heart start to pound in my chest again, racing, out of control. I forced myself to breathe evenly. When I had calmed, I looked up. Death stared at me silently, waiting. I stared back until the silence became too uncomfortable to bear. "Why are you just standing there?" I asked, gulping.

Death didn't reply. *Apparently, that wasn't the right question.* I thought. "Am I allowed to ask questions?" I wondered aloud. "I mean, if I can't ask questions, then how am I going to find out anything? Surely, I can ask questions…"

I realized I was babbling awkwardly and fell silent again. Death stood an armlength away, still waiting.

"Where am I?" I asked very deliberately.

"This a dimension. The dimension of dreams." Death responded calmly. "It connects to all living things. Some humans can access the Dreamscape when they sleep. Not many, but it does happen from time to time."

"And I'm one of those people?" I asked.

Death nodded. "You've had the ability since you were a young child, but you would only flicker in for brief moments and then vanish again. I was never able to catch you to warn you of the dangers."

"What dangers? You mean like the thing that attacked me?" I shuddered.

"Among other things. This is the first time you've stayed for longer than a few moments. You saw how dangerous it can be." I felt Death's penetrating gaze on me. I could see that, whatever was beneath the cowl, her eyes glowed like tiny flames of blue. "I have to admit, you've really kept me on my toes."

"Wait... what? I'm so confused. I always thought Death was stalking me. Are *you* Death, you can't be Death?

Whatever this thing was raised a hand to try and calm me, and even that small gesture made my mind race faster, roiling with noise and confusion. "No, it *has to* be you. You *have* to be Death; you ARE Death.

I have felt that ominous presence in dreams my whole life, it was you! And you say you were trying to warn me?! Why would DEATH be trying to warn me?" My hands balled up into fists, and I felt tears stream from the corners of my eyes. "You're DEATH," I screamed. "I know you! You've been tormenting me my whole life!"

Death turned her head swiftly in my direction. Her eyes exploded in a blue flame. "I am not *The* Death. I am *Your* Death. The Death you're thinking about, the one I serve, is very busy. Make no mistake, I will collect your soul when your appointed time comes. But until your appointed time comes, I will stand as the guard at the gate, your defender from all other evils that exist in the Dreamscape, or those that come from the soul dimension."

"So… you are my protector?" I asked

"I am the protector of your destiny. If your time is tomorrow, then I will come tomorrow. If it's in a hundred years, then I will collect you in a hundred years. That is my job." Her eyes flashed with blue intensity.

"Is my time tomorrow?" I asked timidly. I wasn't challenging her; it was my fear talking.

"It is not for you to know. There is a time, there is a place, until then I will protect the thread of your life."

I paused, taking it all in. Her eyes returned to the soft blue glow I was familiar with. "And you don't have to call me Death if it makes you uncomfortable.

My name is Ophelia. Death is just a title."

I gaped at her. "Excuse me?"

"I prefer Ophelia. My name is Ophelia, I don't actually like being called Death." She looked at me silently.

I looked back and realized, Death was scary, but Ophelia wasn't. She felt right.

"So, Ophelia… What do you look like? Or are you allowed to show me?" I asked hesitantly.

The cowl rippled for a moment. Was she chuckling? "No Dreamer has ever asked before," she responded with a light voice. "My appearance changes from day to day. It depends on what the Dreamer is expecting. You, in this case. You are the Dreamer. Given how panicked you were, I'd bet I look like a skeleton in a dark robe."

"Well, the dark robe and hood is right, but not the skeleton from what I can see," I responded.

"I can lower my cowl, but I really don't know what you'll see. Maybe Anubis if you're into the Egyptian stuff. Most likely a skull. Probably better to leave it up for the time being. I don't want to freak you out again."

"Ok," I replied, "But just so you know, Anubis would be cool."

This time I heard it, she did laugh, but she did not lower her hood.

"What was that thing you fought off earlier?" I felt I was calm enough now to ask sensible questions.

Ophelia's voice became grim. "That was a Haunt. They're part of the Dreamscape. They're fragments of nightmares that coalesce into something more. They bring terror and loathing, and feed off the emotions it generates. They're not the only thing dangerous here, not even the worst really."

"Excuse me? What's worse? It seemed pretty bad to me." I asked, eyes wide.

"The worst is the Soul Snatchers. If a Dreamer enters the Dreamscape when their Death is sleeping, a Soul Snatcher can sneak in with them."

Suddenly I heard a moan in the distance, like the very fabric of my dream was in pain; low, rumbling, pushing though me into my very soul. Ophelia grabbed my hand, "We must go. Now."

I pulled back. "Wait, is that it? Is that the Soul Snatcher?"

"We can't stay here, it's not safe," she said. And for the first time I heard a hint of fear.

"I have no idea what's safe in this world, but if I don't know what I'm fighting, then nowhere is safe." I stared at her, determined not to move. I'd been helpless in this Dreamscape since I got here, but that was going to end.

"Soul Snatchers," she began, then paused. "They are the only creatures that can defeat Death."

"Defeat Death? How is that even possible?" I asked.

Ophelia paused again, trying to collect her thoughts. It occurred to me she'd never had to explain this to anyone before, so I waited patiently. "As I told you, each Dreamer has a personal Death. In this case, the Dreamer is you, and I am Your Death. I am also your protector until your time comes."

"Yes, I know this," I exclaimed. "You've already told me about that."

"Death is diligent," she continued. "But even Death must rest. We sleep, yes, we sleep during those times when you are awake and not here with us in the Dreamscape, but there are rare times when a Dreamer might enter the Dreamscape when her personal Death is sleeping." Ophelia paused.

My own personal fear began to rise again. "And?" I asked, pushing down that part of me that screamed that I didn't want to know.

"And when that happens, there is a fracture in the Dreamscape, a door opens and that's when the Soul Snatcher enters your world, this world, the world of all Dreamers."

"And what happens then?" I asked.

She looked at me evenly, "I think the name of the creature gives you that answer."

235

"That moan we heard earlier, is that one of them?" I asked with some trepidation.

"Yes, from the other side of the door, but that's not why we need to move. That Haunt you encountered, it's not the only one, and though they are not as powerful as a Soul Snatcher, they are still dangerous."

"But this is only a dream!" I said. "My real body is still back there, in that hospital bed, right?"

"If you are killed in your dream, your body follows your spirit, and you are dead in your world. Now come, we have to move." Ophelia started walking out of the clearing. I didn't know what else to do, I didn't want to be alone, so I followed.

"But won't the Haunt follow us?" I asked, catching up to her as I looked around half expecting it to pop out of the trees.

"Yes, I'm counting on it." Ophelia replied.

"What?!"

"Haunts are relentless. It has your scent; it has to feed. It won't stop until we kill it."

"We? Kill it?" Another wave of panic welling up in my throat. "I've never killed anything in my life."

Ophelia shook her head. "If I could send you home, I would, but your body isn't waking up right now. A Haunt is powerful, but not impossible to kill. They're dangerous, and fast, but kind of stupid if I'm being honest." Ophelia strode onward, her eyes scanning our surroundings. She was looking for something. "What did you do, that you aren't waking up?"

"Ah…," I stammered. Not wanting to talk about it. "Ah – I maybe took too much of something. I was *trying* to stay awake! I guess it has the opposite effect when you take too much."

Ophelia gave me a stern look, shaking her head. "It's called an overdose. You know that. And you're just lucky it's not your time yet, or we would be having a very different conversation. Okay, so you'll be here with me until your body wakes up, so you'll have to come along and help. Are you okay with that?"
"Do I have a choice?" I asked, not intending to sound petulant, but somehow it still came out that way. She gave my question more consideration than I expected.

"I can't make you do anything you don't want to do," she said after a few moments. "And as a Dreamer, you have more control over the Dreamscape than you know. But you haven't learned to control or use that skill yet. So, yes. You have a choice, but it would be a lot easier if you agreed to help."

I thought about that. Ophelia seemed like she was being very up-front about everything, something I hadn't experienced much in the adults I knew. My gut was telling me to trust her, even though she looked like Death, but that thing she fought off was also really scary.

"What do you propose?" I asked tentatively.

"Well... that Haunt was fixated on you. I'm sure I could defeat it in a fight, particularly if I ambush it."

"So, what is the plan?" I asked. "To kill this thing, I mean?"

"I need space. I need room to fight it. There's an open area up ahead." Ophelia paused for a moment and suddenly turned to the right, heading up between two large rocks and climbing up an embankment. I followed quickly, realizing that I wasn't in any way out of breath or tired. This was still a dream, and yet so real. Ophelia paused at the top and looked back. "Are you coming? It's just over here."

I couldn't help smiling to myself. She looked like Death, scythe and all, but she sounded like an annoyed, but honest high school teacher. "Coming." I clambered over the embankment. The sight on the other side was amazing. It stretched from the forest edge in all directions in front of me.

"You want us to cross a desert?" I asked, my mouth felt parched just thinking about it.

"We only need to go about a hundred yards further. From there I will have clear visibility in all directions, and plenty of room to fight We already know which direction the Haunt will be coming from," she said, pointing back at the embankment.

I stepped out onto the sand, the grains crunching reassuringly under my feet. Ophelia had already found her spot.

She was looking around nodding her head and seemed satisfied.

"And now what? We wait?"

She turned the scythe over and checked the underside edge of the blade. "Yes. We wait," she responded. Ophelia scanned the horizon, and as the silence became uncomfortable, she asked, "So... what's it like being alive?"

I looked at her in puzzlement, "What do you mean?"

"I've never been to your world. I'm from here. This is obviously very different than your normal existence. I've never even had the opportunity to talk to a human, except in the very moment when I collect them. So, what's it like?"

"Ah... well... I mean... it's... well... first you're born, then you go through childhood, get bigger, grow up...fall in love... get married, get a job... then eventually you get old and then die," I replied, struggling to find the right words. "That's about it... but there's a lot of stuff in all those stages."

Ophelia shook her head, puzzled. "What's the deal with the small ones. They pop in and out of here all the time, but then every time they pop in, they're a little bigger and slower. They start out – usually happy, sometimes mild nightmares, scared of the dark, or loud noises or such. As they get bigger, they get sadder, and their dreams get darker and uglier. Then they get all wrinkled and their dreams get simpler and happier again, until it's finally time for me

JESSICA BRAWNER

to collect them. I've always thought it was strange and kind of sad."

"That's how life works. When you're small, if you're lucky, you have someone that takes care of you, and you don't have much to be afraid of. Then you grow up… I guess technically that's about where I am now… almost grown up, and you have to take care of yourself, and maybe other people. And then when you get old, if you're lucky, someone will take care of you again… I think that's what you're seeing." I had never thought about life in these terms, and it made me uncomfortable.

Ophelia's head shot up. She pointed at the horizon where a dust cloud billowed. "There it is!"

My fear ratcheted up as I watched the swirling cloud. It didn't get any closer though, just zig-zagged back and forth at the horizon.

"It's taunting us. It wants to make you fearful. It can read your fears to a certain extent. The more scared you are, the more powerful it becomes." Ophelia said in a low voice. "This is just a test. It won't come at us this time."

I watched, and her shoulders relaxed, still observing the dust devil, wary and waiting. "So, what's that love thing like?"

I floundered again, surprised at the question. "I'm not really sure. I mean, people talk about it – it's a popular subject. Supposedly you get all weak in the knees, butterflies in your stomach, that sort of thing."

"That sounds uncomfortable," she mused.

"People say it's wonderful," I replied, shrugging.

She looked back at me. "So, you haven't experienced it?"

I shook my head. "Not yet... I don't think so." The thought was unexpectedly sad. "Maybe one day, but it doesn't happen for everyone."

"Look!" I shouted; there it is again. The dust devil was in a new location on the horizon.

Ophelia's head whipped around, and as quickly as it appeared, it vanished. Her eyes grew wider. "Where is it?! Where'd it go? I can't sense it anymore. That's never happened before." She looked at me and paused. "Oh no. You're HERE. All the way here."

"What's that supposed to mean! Of course I'm here!" I said, panicking.

"Usually, it only has little fragments of nightmares and terror to feed on. It will get a sense of a person's fear and can sometimes coalesce. This time it's got an entire buffet."

I looked around frantically trying to spot all the ways it could come at us. It was clear in all directions.

If I couldn't see it, and it wasn't coming from the horizon... I looked down in horror.

"Don't think it!" Ophelia shouted, just as the Haunt burst from the ground at my feet.

I was flabbergasted. I hadn't thought it would appear nearly so fast. The terror was overwhelming, crushing me to my knees in the soft sand. The sand picked up by the Haunt's whirlwind blasted my face, enveloping us in and flinging me into the air. I screamed, and my mouth filled with the dry, dusty debris, choking me.

I heard Ophelia from a great distance. "Block out the terror. You're only making it stronger. It's all in your head. It's not real," she shouted. As I was spun around in the vortex, I saw Ophelia on the ground, scythe in hand. I caught glimpses of her battling something, interspersed with sky and more sand as I was whirled about. Everything was chaos. "You must fight the terror! Block it out." Ophelia's voice was calm, from a great distance, with that weirdly deep resonance to it again.

The longer I spun in the vortex, the multitude of images, things melting at the edges of my vision, the stinging feel of the sand on my skin, the more it reminded me of the one and only time I'd tried Acid. I closed my eyes and curled into a ball to block out the sensations. With my eyes closed I was able to concentrate, and thought to myself – *oh, this feels like flying! Flying is fun. I like having fun.* Still with my eyes closed, I imagined myself soaring and swooping like a bird. Slowly the wind and buffeting sand around me calmed. I could still hear battle below me, and so I opened my eyes to see.

Vertigo. I was high in the sky above Ophelia, who was battling a creature that stood twice her height, with long black flowing robes that whipped in all directions. As I registered what was happening below, I felt myself begin to plummet. The ground rushed towards me, and panic welled up again. The creature looked up at me and smiled, a horrible, toothy smile and seemed to grow taller.

I heard Ophelia's voice again. "Calm yourself, Tamara. Don't panic." I could see that she was tiring and that the creature, now triple in size was pushing her back, away from me.

Suddenly the edges of my vision started to swirl, not with sand, but with psychedelic colors, and I could feel myself being pulled backwards. I could hear voices and beeping machines, and a strange, sterile smell hit my nose. The desert vanished, replaced by my hospital room. I could still taste the sand in my mouth and feel the sting of the wind. "No!" I shouted.

The nurse jumped in surprise and yelled over her shoulder, "Doctor! She's awake!"

"No!" I shouted again. Or tried to. It came out as little more than a frantic whisper. "I have to go back! Ophelia needs me."

The nurse pressed me back down into the bed. "Just rest. You're fine. It's only been a few days," she said, trying to reassure me then yelled again, "Doctor! Hurry!"

I looked around frantically, I was regaining consciousness, leaving the Dreamscape! *But Ophelia…*

The nurse reached for the IV bag to shut off the flow of that drug. The drug that put me into the coma! "No!" I screamed as I knocked her hand away and grabbed the bag, squeezing it as hard as I could. I felt the rush of the liquid as it pulsed into my arm. The room began to swirl, the bright colors returned. Blackness took me, then exploded around me, and I found myself falling.

***

I was back in the Dreamscape, the wind whistling around me as I fell. Ophelia and the Haunt were tiny dots battling far below me. *Oh god, what am I going to do?!* I felt helpless, out of control. But wait! This is *my* Dreamscape. Ophelia said I could control myself and my surroundings. I spread my arms and concentrated on gliding.

She was right! I angled my body and changed direction, aiming right for them. The ground rushed up at me as I got closer. The Haunt struck Ophelia again and again, knocking her to her knees. The creature was stronger and larger, much larger. Why was it still growing without my fear to feed it? Realization dawned on me, it was feeding on Ophelia's fear!

My hands balled up into fists. I became angry, and with that came determination. I was going to stop this thing, but how?

I envisioned a sword, thought about how it would feel, imagined the weight of it. As I did, I felt it come into being. It grew in my hand, rough and about three feet in length, sturdy, but not pretty. It would have to do.

I was unprepared for the shock of impact as I hit the ground and rolled across the sand. With a scream I pushed myself forward, charging at the Haunt. I don't know if it heard me, I didn't care. Ophelia saw me charging toward it and quickly moved to her side, distracting the creature. Without thinking, I swung the sword upwards under the Haunt's right arm, slamming the crude blade into his ribs. It spun in surprise, looking down at me. My sword had been ineffective, it didn't cut. The creature didn't bleed, but it paused, and that was all Ophelia needed. In one graceful motion, her scythe followed a perfect arc, slicing off his left arm then pulling upward to sever his neck. She looked over to meet my eyes, as the creature fell to the ground and disintegrated in a puff of smoke.

"That was quite impressively dramatic," she said, then smiled. "Stupid. But decidedly effective. You could have been killed. What were you thinking?" she said, concern tinging her voice.

"To be honest, I wasn't thinking. You were right. I just thought about what I needed, and it was there. I could fly! And that sword! It just came from nowhere.

"No, I mean why did you come back?" she asked. "You could have escaped. You could have gone back to your world."

I blinked my eyes, not understanding the question. "Um. I had to come back, I had to help you."

My response seemed to take her by surprise. "Thank you. I... thank you. But be careful, because if you die here, you die in your world too."

'That would be 'need to know' information." Looking around I asked with some trepidation, "So is it dead?"

Ophelia shrugged slightly. "Dead is overstating it. The Haunt was made up of fragments of your fear. It's been shattered, and it will not bother us unless it manages to re-form, and that's up to you." Ophelia smiled. "I doubt we'll run into that one again."

She was right. A part of me felt like I should be heaving my guts up in the sand, but my body wasn't reacting that way. The terror I had felt only moments before was entirely gone, and I felt remarkably normal. Moreso even than I did in my day-to-day life. That Haunt was never returning.

Trying to sound nonchalant I said, "Will I remember any of this when I wake up?"

Ophelia studied me. "Yes. You will wake up and remember what happened, clearly. Not like a dream. And when you come back, you'll know where you are."

"When I come back?" I asked, whipping my head around to look at her sharply, all nonchalance dropped. I was curious about this place, but I wasn't sure I wanted to come back. It was clearly both dangerous and scary, but Ophelia wasn't. She wasn't at all what I thought she would be and that made the Dreamscape different.

246

"Yes," she chuckled. "When. It's very rare, but once you've been here, you are assured to return. Not every time you sleep. Not even all that often. The circumstances have to be just right. But Dreamers always return."

Tamara frowned. What Ophelia was saying made her uncomfortable. "But I'm only here because of the drugs, and I don't want to do that anymore."

Ophelia shook her head. "No, that's not what brought you here. You've always been able to enter here, and the drugs were your way of fighting it. Because you were scared. But dreams are what you make of them. The drugs created your fear, and your fear created the Haunt. But – perhaps when you return to your body, you will no longer be afraid of going to sleep?"

I replied, "I don't the drugs anymore. I never want the drugs again."

"And you'll never need them. The Dreamscape is always here, it always has been."

A huge weight lifted from my shoulders. The thing that had terrified me my whole life - the thought that I was being chased by Death, and that Death was waiting for me every time I closed my eyes. This was true and not true. Death was waiting for me every time I went to sleep – and Death was not who or what I thought it was.

Ophelia was my protector, was kind, caring, and had a pretty good sense of humor.

Without warning I suddenly felt the colors around me swirl again, I was waking up, I knew it. I looked at Ophelia. She looked back at me and smiled…

I felt a hand shaking my shoulder. The noises and smells of a hospital were all around me. I opened my eyes and found myself in my hospital bed once again. Despite what had happened, this was the first time in years that I had woken up without being terrified. My parents were there waiting at my bedside, my mother was holding my hand. I looked up them and smiled, "I think everything will be okay now."

And that's how Death became my friend.

The End

You're getting sleepy – that's normal. That whole last story was about sleep. The coziness and warmth are making you a bit drowsy. Only a chapter to go, and then I can show you the inner sanctum of my collection. You'll get to experience it first-hand. Only a few ever make it that far – to see my permanent collection. It's what you came here for after all.

We're nearing the end now. This last story is a strange one – not particularly comfortable, though I hope you are. You've been here with us all day now, and the twilight is setting in.

I imagine your skin is starting to feel dry and a bit papery, having been in front of the fire all day. One last story to read before I take you to your resting place.

I'll be curious to read how "Death Dreams" affects you. I wonder what your choice would be."

JESSICA BRAWNER

DEATH DREAMS
DREAMSCAPE 2

The Dreamscape portal changed, melting, and running together. It was disorienting. I took a moment for my eyes to adjust. The Dreamscape, necessary for the survival of the human psyche, bowed to no man ... or woman, and followed its own laws. Few but the Dreamers could find their way here, even though the Dreamscape touched every living thing on the planet.

In the twenty-one years since my first adventure into the Dreamscape, I had returned more times than I could count. Each time was different and exciting. Each time, Ophelia, my own 'Personal Death' was there to meet me. She was the guardian of my destiny. She knew when I would die, the time and date. That was her job, but until then she was staunch protector of my soul.

I smiled with amusement remembering when I had found out that, while Ophelia was *My* Death, I was not her only soul to protect. At the time I had been upset, disappointed, and a little bit selfish. I wanted to keep Ophelia for myself. "But you're the only one who knows this world exists!" She had reassured me. "You're the only one who can fully experience the Dreamscape. The others dart in and out in their sleep, unaware of this reality. Unaware of the realms they create. You're the only one in my care who experiences your Dreamscape as reality. And you're the only one I call friend."

It was that last part that made me choke up. Death... at least *My* Death, was my friend. During the many times I visited, I saw other souls flickering in and out, as she had described, not knowing that their Dreamscape was a world of their creation, just as rich and complicated as their waking world. The wakey wakey world as I liked to call it. It made Ophelia laugh, so I kept calling it that. Have you ever heard Death laugh? It's beautiful.

The drugs and fear that had driven my first adventure to the Dreamscape were a thing of the past. I no longer took those drugs, and I certainly didn't fear sleep anymore. I had created a life for myself in the wakey wakey world. True love still eluded me, but there was no longer the pressure to find it. I had learned to appreciate the struggle and efforts my adoptive parents had gone through to provide for me.

We grew closer, and I cherished my moments with them. As I approached my 40's I wondered if I would ever take the step my parents had, to foster children and help those like me, who had been orphaned at an early age.

Now, I was being pulled into the Dreamscape, heading back to visit my friend. I wished I had more control over when I could visit. Most often, the Dreamscape brought me when it thought I needed to be here. My Dreamscape was a creation of my soul, part of my very being and while it wasn't precisely alive, or conscious, it could make it's wishes known. Over time I had learned that I could control much of it while I was here but getting here by myself was not within my power. I could only come when it called to me. It's a bit hard to explain. Have you ever had those times when you haven't talked to someone in a long time, but you just know you should give them a call? It's like that. It isn't Ophelia calling to me, it isn't me wanting to go, it's my own Dreamscape telling me it's time for a visit.

These thoughts and memories flashed through me as the Dreamscape portal opened the colors running together. Fragments of the Dreamscape remained the same every time I came here, but other parts changed, sometimes dramatically. Every time the colors were vibrant and alive.

This time, when I stepped into the Dreamscape, I was about halfway up a cliff side, standing on a small promontory of rock. Mountains loomed above me, and a lake stretched out, colored by moonlight. Something was different though. The colors were... dingy, almost tarnished. The air was murky, and I could not see as far as I was accustomed to. Air pollution was not a thing in the Dreamscape. I looked around for Ophelia, eager to see her again. She had never failed to be here when I arrived, no matter where the Dreamscape deposited me, and she would know what was going on.

"Don't you get tired of visiting me child?" the sonorous voice of Ophelia asked.

I turned. She was there, and tonight the Dreamscape had decided she would appear as an old woman, tall and upright, but frail, wearing a shockingly day-glow pink hood and carrying her black banded scythe. Ophelia's appearance changed every time I came here, sometimes dramatically, based on my state of mind. I remember the first time I ever entered the Dreamscape; she looked like the classic figure of Death – black robes, scythe, very scary. But I had been feeling pretty good lately, so her appearance as a frail old woman was a little strange. I shrugged. Maybe there was something on her mind. There were only two things that never changed - her scythe, and her eyes. If I looked into her eyes for too long the bright blue flames in their depths would capture and consume me.

"How could I possibly tire of you? And besides, the Dreamscape called me here again."

Ophelia looked me up and down. "What does it feel like?" In this body the normal timber of her voice seemed different, less firm, raspier.

"When the Dreamscape calls?" I asked.

She nodded. "I've never felt it – not from the waking world side of course."

It was weird hearing her call it the waking world. That was never how we referred to it. Something must be on her mind. I shrugged it off. She'd get around to telling me what she wanted to talk about in due time. "It varies. Sometimes it's a gentle tap on a thick wooden door, and sometimes it feels like it's using a sledgehammer on a pane of glass," I replied. "Regardless, it's not something you ignore, when it calls. Today, it felt like there was great urgency."

"Huh." She replied, as if noting new information. "I wonder how it works – or why it works that way. It would be an interesting thing to know." Ophelia said, her head tilting at a birdlike angle as she looked at me.

I shrugged. "I hadn't really thought much about it since it's not something I can control." I studied her. I'd known Ophelia for years. It wasn't unusual for her to ask questions about how things here impacted me, or what it was like being alive, she experienced it all from such a very different perspective, but... "Is everything okay? Are you feeling okay?" I asked her as I turned to look out over the spangled mountains.

"Whatever do you mean?" she replied. "I'm Death. It's not like I have feelings."

"It just seems like something's bothering you, and I wanted to make sure there was nothing wrong." I replied. Ophelia hated being called Death. It was a title, not a name, and for her to refer to herself as Death... something must really be upsetting her today.

A pulse of light flashed from one of the peaks, paused, flashed again. Like lightening hitting something. Momentarily distracted, pushing my concern to the back of my mind, I pointed to the mountain. "Did you see that?" More lightning flashed in the distance over the same peak.

"That's unusual. Let's investigate." She held out a long, bony wrist and when I touched it, we were flying.

We flew down the mountain, the ground speeding by below us, the tips of trees within arm's reach. Suddenly we were in the clear, soaring above the lake. Ophelia had my arm in almost a painful grasp as we sailed through the murky air. "What's Death like?" I asked, as we flew. *The* Death was an entity that I had never met, and hoped never to meet, but I was still curious about him. This was a question I had asked Ophelia in the past. We'd had several lively discussions on the topic. The first time I'd met her I'd thought *She* was Death but I never forgot the way she answered that question the first time. "*I am not The Death. I am Your Death. The Death you're thinking about, the one I serve, is very busy.*" She never failed to remind me that she was *My* Death, not *The* Death, and the distinction was very important to her.

"Oh, being Death is a lot of responsibility. I have so many souls I have to take care of. You're my favorite though. You're the only one who comes to visit me. I've always wondered how you've been able to come and go so regularly." Ophelia said, smiling over at me.

I was shocked by the wrongness of her response and was instantly on guard, concern and fear warring with each other. Was she under some sort of duress, trying to communicate it by saying something so outrageous? Lightning struck the mountaintop again, and I heard a moan, as if some giant creature was in pain, just on the other side of the peak. Something was very off tonight. The very fabric of the Dreamscape seemed wounded or damaged.

We were nearing the peak. The tall trees below us had given way to alpine tundra – a place full of boulders, where nothing but lichen and ground cover would grow. Here though, anything was possible. We were close enough to the ground that I pulled myself out of Ophelia's grasp. Falling is never pleasant, but I was prepared for it and rolled with the impact. I hadn't accounted for the slope thought, and rolled painfully downhill until I came up against a boulder. The she landed lightly beside me.

"Child, what were you thinking, flinging yourself down a boulder field like that. You could have been killed!" She asked me, her face a picture of concern.

I looked around, trying to think of something to say. Why had I flung myself out of Ophelia's grasp? She was just acting so strange and out of character. "This area reminds me of the rocky meadow you took me to when I told you my mother had died," I replied, saying the first thing that came to mind. I was lying through my teeth – my mother was very much alive and well when I had seen her two days ago, but my instincts were on high alert.

"Oh. I'm so sorry. I didn't think about what this place would bring to mind," she said consolingly. "Let's get you out of this area of unpleasant memories."

My eyes widened in horror. Ophelia knew very well that my mother was alive, so whoever or whatever this was, it wasn't her. It saw the expression on my face and spat out a curse word.

"You know – don't you," it said.

"Well, you certainly just confirmed it," I replied. "Where is Ophelia?"

Whatever this thing was turned and smiled, a crooked, disturbing smile. "Shall I drop my mask?" the not-Ophelia cackled.

"If you don't mind…" I replied, mind working frantically. *If I'm here, and Ophelia hasn't come to meet me, and something took on Ophelia's semblance….* Ophelia was in trouble somewhere. Maybe that's why the Dreamscape had called to me so loudly. She needed my help!

"With pleasure. This form itches," it replied.

Faster than I thought possible, Ophelia's form had vanished, and a horror stood before me. I shuddered with revulsion. A giant mass of oozing black tentacles, more than I could count, topped by a bulbous head. Eyes, hundreds of eyes looked down at me, each blinking at its own rate, all red-rimmed and inflamed. A gash of a mouth split the middle. It held the mockery of Ophelia's scythe at its side and swung it at me. Without thinking, I immediately conjured a sword, pulling it from the fabric of the Dreamscape, just in time to parry the creature's swipe. Ophelia and I had practiced both conjuring the sword and my using it, nearly every time I visited the Dreamscape. I could hear her voice in my head, "This is not always a safe place, and you must know how to defend yourself." If I died here, in my Dreamscape, I would die in all worlds.

"What are you?" I asked in revulsion. It continued its attack, first feinting to the right, then pressing me hard, forcing me to back up. I moved uphill, toward the summit, taking the high ground where I had the advantage. This thing was both faster and bigger than me.

"Can you not guess?" it replied, in a grating voice. "I've waited so long for this. Planned for this. Watching you. Watching you come and go here in the Dreamscape. Unlike anyone has done before. Figuring out what calls to you… Waiting until things were arranged just so, so that I might enter…"

"Ah! So that's why you were asking all those questions about what it felt like to be called here," I said, realization dawning, followed by absolute horror.

"Of course. There are many more Dreamers, souls I can feed on. Just waiting for me to call them – now that I know how." It cackled evilly. "I will feast well, and for years to come."

Once again, the creature feinted to the side, allowing me to take another advantageous spot, between rocks that protected my flanks. Though it was bigger and stronger, it didn't seem to know anything about tactics. I moved backward, uphill again, it followed, vulnerable to my counter attacks. "You could have killed me at any time… why bring me here?" I asked.

"Oh. I will have your soul, never fear. Or… perhaps DO fear. Quite a lot. Your fear tastes so sweet. But I only wish to reunite you with your Death before the end." Its voice oozed over me as my mind tried frantically to put all the pieces together. My arm burned, as I parried swipes from the scythe. The creature was fast, but it was giving me all the advantage of position and movement. That didn't make sense. Suddenly I realized; it was *giving me the advantage!* Of course! It was deliberately moving me in the direction it wanted by making me believe I was winning. It was *herding* me! But where? And why? We were near the mountaintop. For some reason it wanted me up there. We were close now, and another bolt of lightning split the sky. Illuminating a flat stone, laid out like an alter or a bier with a body laid atop it.

Between the flashes of light and darkness I made out a shape, a figure sprawled on a flat rock in an open area, silent. Unmoving. My heart fluttered in shock. It was Ophelia!

"Ophelia!" I called, barely blocking another relentless blow from the creature. "Ophelia!" I yelled louder. She didn't move, she didn't look at me. She was immobile as if dead. But that wasn't possible! How do you kill Death?

I tried move closer to her. The creature I fought knew what I was doing but didn't seem to care, as if it already knew it had won this battle.

I saw it! A slight movement, she still breathed, but slowly, as if asleep.

"What have you done to her?!" I screamed at the horror attacking me.

"I?" the monstrosity seemed to giggle with glee. "I have done nothing to her. She sleeps, as she does. When her Dreamers aren't here, when she is her weakest, your Death sleeps. And she cannot awaken while you are here. I have the power now!"

"Okay – she can't wake up if I'm here, got it." I was desperate, I had to find something, anything, to fight back. "But why bring me here? Why not just kill me when I appeared?" I shouted, frantically trying to buy time.

"She didn't tell you, did she? Of course not, she didn't think she needed to know. The Dreamscape doesn't call to you when she's sleeping. Unless someone makes it cry out in pain."

"You attacked the Dreamscape so it would call to me?" I asked, horrified.

"I've tried many things, many times. None worked. Until now. And here you are. You can only die in the presence of your Death. And now I shall have you both," it cackled, swinging its scythe toward my head.

I ducked and thrust my sword toward the eye facing me, plunging into its wet goo. It pulled back and another replaced it. So many tentacles with those damn eyes, I'd have to get in closer to hit it, or …

I'd never practiced with a longsword, just the short sword I was using now, but this was the Dreamscape; MY Dreamscape – I could control certain things. With that thought, my sword grew an extra foot, without adding any weight. The blade gleamed, reflecting the lightning. I lunged again and scored a gash across one of the tentacles behind the eyes, and the creature screamed in pain. The earsplitting shriek reverberated inside my head, pushing me to my knees. That meant it could be wounded, it could be killed! But how?

Suddenly I was aware of a whisper in my head. Something that sounded faint but began to coalesce into words. It was Ophelia's voice, quietly speaking. She was reaching out to me, our spirits connecting as they had so many times before, I glanced at her body again, still where it was. But she was speaking to me! "You fight the Soul Snatcher, child!"

That shook me for a moment; she had mentioned Soul Snatchers were the worst horror of the Dreamscape, a more dangerous foe than any of my nightmares could conjure. This was one of them?

"Listen to me," Ophelia's voice went on. "If a Dreamer enters the Dreamscape when their Death is sleeping, a Soul Snatcher can sneak in with them."

"It came in with me?" I asked, stumbling to my feet and looking around as the creature continued to force me backwards toward the stone bier. "But why can't you help me?"

"I am here child, but very weak." Her voice was a whisper in my thoughts, barely there. I could feel the calm, the poise through this bond. It felt like her. But I began to panic. I was being overwhelmed, the Soul Snatcher no longer allowed me the advantages that directed me here, it was now fighting with its full potential.

"Ophelia, what do I do?" I asked frantically. "I can't defeat this thing! I need your help! Please!"

"You must defeat it. If you do not, it will kill you, steal your soul, and then kill me. And if that happens it will feast on all the other souls I protect. It has learned how to call the Dreamers here and it will devour each one. That must not happen," she said weakly through our bond. "You must stop it for them… for me…."

"But how!" I asked, frantically parrying another swipe from the scythe.

"You must kill me." She said.

My heart stopped, my breath stopped, I almost fell.

"Tamara, my dearest friend. There's only one way to defeat a Soul Snatcher. It feasts on the Dreamers, but I am their path to this creature. My death will banish it, will break that connection. You must kill me." Ophelia's body on the bier twitched as if she was trying to wake up, or was caught in a bad dream, but her words had been clear.

"I … I can't kill you. You're my friend. You're my *best* friend. I don't know what I would do without you," I said, choking back tears. I ducked behind a large boulder to try and get a moment's respite from the Soul Snatcher. My arm was tiring, and I felt as if the energy was being drained from me, while Ophelia's words battered my mind.

"You must. There is no other way."

"I can't! I don't know what I would do without you! Ophelia, please, there has to be another way. What will happen to all the other Dreamers you protect? Who will guard their destiny?"

"You. You will protect them. If you kill me, you become me, you take my place and take on my role of protecting the other Dreamers." Ophelia's voice in my head was sounding weaker now. "I know how much it is to ask of you, but you must Tamara, before I lose the strength to help you at all."

"I know you're talking to her," the Soul Snatcher said to me as it leaned in, slicing the scythe upwards toward my head. I dodged to the side, my blade diverting it, but I was getting weaker, it sensed that, I could tell. "It will do you no good," it stated calmly, as a fact. "Give in now, accept the sleep of oblivion that I offer you."

It slammed a tentacle into my legs, knocking me down. I rolled to avoid another attack and came up on my feet. I was unsteady, my legs were weak, barely keeping me up.

"Ophelia, I'll become a Death? What will happen to me in the wakey wakey world?" I asked, shaking. Facing the thought of killing my friend was unbearable. I wasn't sure I was strong enough to do that. Ophelia had saved me from myself when I was younger, the first time I came here, and was the dearest, most loyal friend I had ever known.

"You will not ever be able to return. Your body will die, uninhabited by its soul. But you will be here to protect the souls and call them to their final time of rest. Please Tamara, you must do this, or countless others will be in peril... Please..." her voice in my head was growing weaker. I had seen some of the other souls Ophelia protected over the years. They were defenseless here, flitting in and out without awareness, easily caught by the monstrosity that continued to hammer away at me.

I couldn't let them be caught by this thing. I didn't want Ophelia's soul to be caught by this thing either. I knew what I had to do, but knowing didn't make it any easier. "What happens to you when you die?" I asked her.

"Tamara. It is not for any of us to know what lies beyond. My dear friend, thank you for everything we have shared. It is time," she replied calmly.

Darting out from behind the boulder I sprinted for the bier and Ophelia's body, tears streaming down my face. Reaching her, I tore the hood down to stare at my beloved friend, every pore in my body fearful of what was to come. She was there, beautiful, serene, and she wore my face. She was me. Tears filled my eyes, as I choked back sobs.

I heard the Soul snatcher slithering up behind me. "No! You both will be mine!"

Laying my sword across her throat, I kissed her forehead and bid my dearest friend goodbye, watching as my blade ended her existence. As the last vestiges of life left her body, the Soul Snatcher screamed. "Nooo!

My sword turned to scythe – the ever-sharp scythe of Death. Spinning around I swung it, slicing upward, catching the creature off its guard. I felt the blade slice cleanly through it as I screamed. "I banish you. Begone! And know that I did not kill you… my friend did!" Unknown power flooded through me, and a grim, dark portal opened, sucking the pieces of the foul creature back into the dark dimension.

My ears rang with the sudden silence. I heard sobbing, and realized it was coming from me as I fell to my knees facing Ophelia's bier. Sunrise glimmered in the distance, the pale golden light that heralds dawn. "I will miss you, so much." I said, my heart heavy with sadness, as tears streamed down my face. I could feel the souls in my charge, and I had no idea what came next.

I was alone and afraid, and I was Death.

The End

Well, Iktómi – our newest addition to the collection is complete. The ink is dry, and you've done a wonderful job with the binding. Such care and craftmanship. This one is so full of life, it will enrich my collection greatly. The fresh binding is vibrant and soft to the touch. I was right with that last cup of tea – the ink is strong all the way to the end. They had many adventures before they arrived here, and I look forward to getting to know them better. I'm so glad they came to visit.

I shall shelve them in the adventure section, and perhaps our next visitor will enjoy the stories of their life. I do hope it's not too long until someone else comes by. Just this one lovely individual has given me the energy to repair the roof, but the stairs still need tending to. I must keep the collection safe so that they remain a source of wonder and inspiration to all who come to visit.

I wonder what stories our next visitor will call forth.

JESSICA BRAWNER

ABOUT THE AUTHOR

Jessica Brawner is a Los Angeles based author who writes both fiction and non-fiction and has been an active part of the Sci-fi, Fantasy, geek community for most of her adult life. She has a passion for teaching others and regularly speaks at conventions and events on the business side of writing. She is an avid reader and began writing professionally in 2014.

Visit her website, www.jessicabrawner.com or find her online on Facebook and Twitter @JABrawner

Read on for an exciting excerpt from the first Novel in the Adventures of Captain Jac

The First Sin

*T*he *Indiana*, my pride and joy, limped into the Palermo airfield in Sicily on its last dregs of fuel. The crew looked haggard; the airship was barely holding together; no one had been paid in months. If we didn't get a job, we would be dead in the air. Palermo was new territory for us, but I had some leads.

Today was also my first mate Tyler's birthday, so the crew and I scraped together the few remaining coins we had to take him out for a night on the town.

Even from the street the bar stank of cheap alcohol, sweat and too many drunken brawls. It was perfect. We staggered into the tavern laughing at one of Nina's rare jokes; the sign outside had a picture of a tankard on fire. *The Flaming Mug.*

The crew herded Tyler over to the bar, calling for a round of drinks. I followed, scanning the room to see if my contact had arrived. I hadn't dealt with him before – Zacharias, one of our former clients, provided the introduction. He knew our skillsets – discretion, disguise, misdirection, mechanical genius, procuring the hard to get.

Two men sat in one shadowy corner talking, their voices muted. At another private table a merchant ate his dinner, looking about with tired eyes. A group of young men sat on the other side of the room toasting boisterously and tossing dice. A crowd around the bar awaited drinks from harried-looking bar maids. I smiled and joined the crowd.

When I went back for my second glass of wine a barmaid slipped a note under my glass and glanced towards a man sitting at the other end of the bar. He was younger than I expected, dark haired and dark eyed with a quick smile. I raised an eyebrow in his direction and he nodded. I smiled at the barmaid and slid a few coins her direction, picking up the wine and the note.

11:30 tonight, upstairs, room five.

Chuckling, I rolled my eyes. This was probably my contact, and not some local who hoped for an exciting tumble between the sheets. I had made that mistake once before though, much to everyone's amusement. I glanced at the clock; it was only ten. Looking back, the man was gone.

Joining my crew, I slid the note over to Nina. "What do you think? Job or love note?"

Nina chuckled, "If it's a love note, I'll buy the next round."

I grinned wryly. "And if it's our contact, next round is on me. I wish Zacharias had provided a better description. As much as I hate to pull you away from the party, I'll need a lookout."

Nina grinned. "Of course. And if he is expecting a tumble in the sheets, won't he be surprised to have us both there."

Glancing at her sideways I said, "You're impossible, you know that, right?"

She laughed a deep, throaty laugh. "It's why you keep me around."

Tyler was having a grand time with a willing barmaid on one knee and another who made sure his tankard stayed filled. Marie chatted with the men at the adjacent table, clearly enjoying herself. I'd occasionally hear terms like "overdrive," "inert gas" and "alloy." I enjoyed tinkering with mechanics myself, and I was decent at it, but Marie was a genius. She knew what it took to keep an airship flying, and her miniature clockwork creations were marvelous.

Henri, our ship's doctor, was as out of place as anyone could be at a bar. His button-down shirt and polished shoes stood out among the rough wear of the patrons. He stared at Marie, longing and jealousy flitting across his face. I smiled into my cup. The crew were laying bets on when those two would finally get together.

It took me a while to find Seamus, our security specialist and supply chief. He was standing at the center of a knot of young men, playing darts. I watched as he flung the fletched objects carelessly. To the untrained eye it looked like he was barely paying attention to the game, but each dart hit the center of the subsequent wedge, spiraling from the outer edge to the inner bullseye.

I shook my head with a grin. Those young men would go home tonight somewhat lighter in their pockets.

At eleven fifteen I caught Nina's eye and nodded towards the stairs. She extricated herself from a group of admirers and joined me.

After the noise in the common room, the upstairs was quiet. The hall ran the entire length of the building, with rooms on either side, the wooden floors worn shiny with years of foot traffic. Gaslights flickered along the walls, their cool blue light illuminating the sparse decor.

Room five was halfway down on the right. I took a moment to compose myself before I entered. Nina leaned against the wall next to the door, the one nearest the exit. As I raised my hand to knock, the door swung open.

A small sitting room greeted me. The walls were a soothing green blue, nothing too garish or exciting— there was no bed, only a modest table with chairs off to the side. The gas lamps around the room burned with a warm, welcoming glow.

The man from the bar was sitting on the far side of the room. "Come in *ma belle* please, Captain. My name is Franco." He sat on a small couch, foot resting on one knee, drinking what appeared to be brandy. Several men stood around, looking like they would rather be downstairs in the bar.

"Jac." I said as I entered, Nina a half-step behind and to my right.

The man's eyes crinkled in the corners, and he smiled. "I see you brought a drinking companion for my men. Please, help yourself. The brandy is quite decent."

I nodded to Nina, and she joined the group as I sat on the couch opposite our potential employer, taking him in. Dark hair, dark eyes held a twinkle of humor; he exuded an air of careless confidence as he dangled a brandy glass callously by the tips of his fingers. Another glass sat on the low table between us. He raised an eyebrow at my scrutiny.

"Well Captain, do you like what you see?" He winked.

"I'm more interested in finding out if I like what I hear," I replied coolly. "I understand you might have a job."

He laughed and sat up, leaning forward. "Direct, I like it. Your reputation said as much. Yes, I have a job, if you're willing to take it. It may be beyond even your crew's considerable ability, though." He didn't quite sneer, and his tone wasn't condescending enough to

274

take offense at, but it raised my hackles.

"Try me," I replied. "I'll be the judge of what we take, or don't."

"You have handled jobs involving heads of state before."

It was a statement, not a question, which surprised me. Franco was more well informed, than I thought.

"The job is quite dangerous, and I wish impress upon you the delicacy of the matter and make sure you are capable of completing it, should we come to an agreement."

I raised an eyebrow. "Are you trying to bait me, monsieur? I can't make a fair assessment of the job until I know something about it."

He leaned back hands extended. "I would never bait someone as lovely as you, Jac. Your reputation precedes you, and because my client knows how risky this job is, he is willing to pay a considerable amount to have it done. Your handling of the Stuart Sapphire heist, one of the crown jewels of Europe, is well known in certain circles. That was deftly done. This will require even more ingenuity."

The small hairs rose on the back of my neck. Zacharias had not known about that job. "Ah. So, we will not be working for you." I nodded, making up my mind.

"When your employer wishes to meet and discuss the job, please be back in touch. I like to know who I'm working for." I stood to leave, catching Nina's eye and gesturing to the door.

I was halfway to the door when he said, "Captain! At least hear the offer." His voice was tinged with worry. "My employer asked for you specifically, but he deals with no one in person. The rich and powerful do not do their own dirty work."

I smiled to myself. He wanted us. Which gave me all of the negotiating power. I turned back, scowling, pretending reluctance. "Do not waste my time, Franco."

"I have been authorized to pay you a small sum, just to listen to the offer. My employer thought you might be reluctant."

I raised an eyebrow at that. "I will listen, but only because I find you entertaining. You have one minute. Go."

He nodded, breathing a sigh of relief. "Very well. My employer, who wishes to remain nameless, is extremely wealthy and is a collector of rare religious relics. His collection is quite large, but he requires a very special piece, and absolute discretion. The piece he desires is found only in the Vatican. Naturally, given the risk involved, he is quite willing to pay a handsome sum for its retrieval. He is offering two thousand gold pieces."

I looked at Franco with incredulity and started laughing. "You jest. For that sum you could not even convince me to leave port." I narrowed my eyes and leaned forward. "If your employer wishes to hire the best crew for this job then he will have to do better than that."

Franco looked disconcerted and rubbed the back of his neck. "Ten thousand gold," he muttered, just loud enough for me to hear.

My mind went blank for a moment contemplating the sum, as my heart started pounding. Ten thousand gold pieces was enough to buy the ship outright. Deals like this were things you only heard about. It immediately put me on my guard.

I was surprised to hear my voice sounding cool and collected. "That is a more worthy sum, which means he appreciates how dangerous this job is. Make it twenty thousand gold pieces and we will consider it."

Franco didn't even blink when he said, "Done. You drive a hard bargain, Captain."

I understood Franco's original offer then. He had wanted to keep the money for himself. Something was definitely off. No one agreed to that kind of money. I extended my hand to shake his. "I'll let you know tomorrow if we decide to accept."

He did blink at that. "I thought you just..."

I smiled, "I believe I said for twenty thousand gold pieces we would consider it. I will give you my answer tomorrow evening after I've consulted my crew. If we accept, then I will get the details about the item."

Franco's face went through a variety of emotions from surprise to anger, his mouth opening and closing but not knowing what to say. "Captain, I would prefer to get this wrapped up tonight. It is important that I report back to my employer that this has been taken care of."

I nodded. "I'm sure you would, Franco, but I won't do a job this big without the full cooperation and agreement of my crew. As you yourself pointed out, this is not a standard job, and I don't have a standard crew. Shall I meet you back here tomorrow evening, say six o'clock?"

His nostrils flared, and I could see plainly he wanted to refuse me. "Fine. Six o'clock tomorrow. Don't be late."

"And my payment for listening?" I held out my hand and he grimaced. I half thought he had been bluffing, so when he tossed me a small pouch I very nearly missed catching it.

I smiled and tucked it into a pocket in my vest without looking at the contents. "Until tomorrow then. Have a pleasant evening."

Nina followed me into the hall. When we were far enough so I was sure Franco's men wouldn't overhear us, I said, "Round up the crew, get them back to the ship. Now. I need everyone sobered up by tomorrow morning so we can discuss this. I'll settle the bill here."

Nina nodded in her taciturn way. "Aye, Captain. I'll see you at the airship."

At the table I took a moment to open the pouch and spill the contents onto my palm. A dozen tiny diamonds rolled out, one of them falling to the floor. Nina's eyes widened.

"*Merde.*" I carefully poured the contents back into the pouch, hoping no-one but Nina had seen. I didn't want to make a spectacle by searching for the lost one. By the time I got the bar keeper's attention and settled the bill, Nina had the crew out the door and on their way.

Everything was quiet onboard the ship. I took second watch while everyone else turned in for the night. In the small hours of the morning the ship's *grand poche*, the large envelope filled with smaller individual balloons cast shadows on half the deck, creating pools of darkness as a counterpoint to the moon's bright, clear light. The brass vent pipes snaking up through the deck from the engine room below gleamed, winking from the darkness whenever a cloud crossed the moon. Seamus appeared like some mythical creature out of one of his tales, stepping into a beam of moonlight. "I'm here to relieve you, Captain."

I smiled. "I can't sleep anyway Seamus, you may as well go back to bed."

"Jac, if you don't mind my sayin', you didn't look

real pleased when you came downstairs from talking to that fella." Seamus leaned against the airship's railing, looking off into the distance.

"You would be correct in your assumption, *mon ami*. The offer is too good, the messenger was too charming, and the job is more dangerous than any we've taken on yet. I can't quite lay my finger on it, but either his employer is an idiot with too much money; good for us, bad for him. Or there is something going on. Did you notice anything unusual about the pub?" I leaned back, elbows propped on the railing, staring across the deck.

Seamus hmphed. "They had painted recently, but that hardly seems suspicious. I dinna see the messenger. Do you want to talk about the offer?"

"Tomorrow when the crew is all together is soon enough," I said, stifling a yawn. "Seems I am tired. I'm going get some sleep. I'll see you in the morning."

Seamus nodded. "Aye. Have a good night, Captain."

I didn't bother lighting the lamps in my cabin, just kicked off my boots and loosened my leather vest enough to wriggle free. The feel of the night air through my thin shirt was chilly but pleasant. Brushing out my hair I tried to pinpoint what was bothering me about the job without success.